COSTLY FREEDOM

To: Aidan

COSTLY FREEDOM
written by Terry Webb

Terry Webb
March, 2010

TATE PUBLISHING & *Enterprises*

Costly Freedom
Copyright © 2009 by Terry Webb. All rights reserved.

No part of this publication may be reproduced, stored in a retrieval system or transmitted in any way by any means, electronic, mechanical, photocopy, recording or otherwise without the prior permission of the author except as provided by USA copyright law.

The opinions expressed by the author are not necessarily those of Tate Publishing, LLC.

Published by Tate Publishing & Enterprises, LLC
127 E. Trade Center Terrace | Mustang, Oklahoma 73064 USA
1.888.361.9473 | www.tatepublishing.com

Tate Publishing is committed to excellence in the publishing industry. The company reflects the philosophy established by the founders, based on Psalm 68:11,
"The Lord gave the word and great was the company of those who published it."

Book design copyright © 2009 by Tate Publishing, LLC. All rights reserved.
Cover design by Lindsay B. Behrens
Interior design by Jeff Fisher
Illustration by Greg White

Published in the United States of America

ISBN: 978-1-61566-294-4
1. Fiction, African American, Historical
2. Juvenile Fiction, People & Places, United States, African American
09.11.20

DEDICATION

This book is dedicated to the Benedict, Williams, Hepburn, McCullough, and Fletcher descendents, as well as the descendents of former slaves.

ACKNOWLEDGEMENTS

Since my childhood, I have been intrigued and fascinated with a story written by my Aunt Julia about her family's life in Georgia. Julia was the last daughter born to my great-grandparents before my great-grandmother died shortly after the family's return to Georgia from Canada. My grandmother, Lucy Benedict, was born while the Benedict family lived in Canada. Since both my grandfather and my father were advocates for equality and justice, I was puzzled to know more about what could have been the reason General Sherman banished my great-grandfather to Canada. As an author I took the liberty in this story of having my great-grandfather tell his children the reason. I also know only what my Aunt Julia wrote about her oldest brother, Sam, from the perspective of a very young sibling. But I have uncovered in my researching my family roots that Sam eventually chose a career as a pharmacist. I believe the scene of the makeshift hospital ward and the experience of knowing Will's father's brain damage must have had a profound impact on his career choice.

I am grateful for the assistance of the Marietta Museum and its staff, the archivist at St. James Episcopal Church, and the staff of the Kennesaw Mountain Battle Museum. They all provided valuable historical background for *Costly Freedom*. I am also indebted to Joe McTyre who so graciously provided the copyrights for some of the photos and images from *Images of America, Cobb County*. Also I could not have completed this work without the support of the staff of Tate Publishing, the Highlights Foundation and my fellow writers. I owe a special thanks to Kay Collier who first edited the manuscript and to the seventh grade Martin Meylin Middle School students and their teacher, Memory D'Agostino, who provided advice and critique prior to its publication.

FOREWORD

The American Civil War affected Marietta, Georgia, unlike any other war in the past. It was the only war actually fought within the city limits, and the town was left completely unrecognizable from its former splendor. It is hard for us to imagine the degree of devastation and the monumental changes that shook society and turned every former reality into something completely opposite.

The one shining light within the dark cloud of despair was, of course, the end of slavery. All men, women, and children enslaved and treated as less than human were finally free! Records show 3,404 slaves were freed in Cobb County, Georgia. Although some left the area immediately, most remained nearby the only place they had ever called home. Freedom elsewhere did not come with the assurance of a job or shelter. So, many slaves stayed with their former masters with the promise of food and shelter in return for the same work previously performed. Unfortunately, those promises could not be kept as starvation was becoming an epidemic in the area. The farmland that once overflowed with food and cash crops had been destroyed by marching troops and entrenchments and only a small portion could be cultivated. To make matters worse, state and federal armies charged with food distribution refused to give any to former slaveholders. As a result, these newly-freed slaves starved as well. This is the environment from which the town is trying to recuperate when *Costly Freedom* begins. Although it has been two years since the end of the war, the characters in this story aptly show how these prior devastations are still plaguing the area.

Costly Freedom depicts how, despite the newfound freedom, racial tensions and prejudices abounded throughout the nation. Although there was an active Freedman's Bureau office in Marietta, it mostly concentrated on labor rights, not on education. After the war, there was no state or local government money available to rebuild schools, but several private schools opened for white children with the funds to pay tuition. The first public school opened in 1867 for whites only. Mixing black and white children in one school room, as in *Costly Freedom,* did not occur in Marietta until the desegregation of the city schools in 1963 (nine years after the Brown vs. Board of Education decision to desegregate nationally).

In this fictional story, Terry Webb has brought together characters from different areas of the post-antebellum society and has shown how truly complex and difficult life was, even among friends. She has continued to remind us that although our past may not be pretty, it is imperative that we never forget these events. Let us always remember the many struggles we have overcome to evolve into a great nation led by our first black president.

—Amy G. Reed,
Curator, Marietta Museum of History.

INTRODUCTION

> I (cannot) brush aside the magnitude of the injustice done, or erase the ghosts of generations past, or ignore the open wound, the aching spirit that ails this country still.
>
> —Barack Obama, *Audacity of Hope*, 115.

In 2009, Barack Obama took the oath of office as the 44th American elected president of the United States. Many oppressed groups heralded and celebrated this historic event.

African-Americans came to Washington, DC, by the millions, from all over the United States to witness his inauguration. They joined others from around the world who sensed that Martin Luther King's dream of equality for all had at long last come true.

Before the 2008 presidential election, the Protestant Episcopal Church—hoping to ease that pain felt by so many descendents of slaves—led the way for other church denominations by apologizing for their past involvement in the perpetuation of slavery. *What difference would such an apology make?* I wondered. Won't actions speak louder than those words? I believe the election of Barack Obama was the action needed to really erase that generational pain. Michelle Obama, her mother and her children, all descendents of slaves, now live in the nation's cherished White House as the first family of the land. African-Americans can be justifiably proud.

African-Americans, through all their struggles to gain full recognition as citizens, have held onto Martin Luther King's dream that all of us are created equal by God no matter whether one's skin is black, brown, white or yellow. Yet, my great-grandfather, the Reverend Samuel Benedict, who was rector of St. James Church in Marietta, Georgia, prior to, during, and after the Civil War espoused the cause of the confederacy and the right to own slaves. After the passage of the Thirteenth, Fourteenth, and Fifteenth amendments to the US Constitution, even as late as the nineteen-fifties and sixties, many pockets in America were still segregated.

In this story I seek to capture what it was really like for freed slaves after the Civil War, lest we forget the humiliation and suffering that still existed for them after the Emancipation Proclamation had proclaimed them free.

SAM RETURNS

Scenes of blackened fields, broken wagon wheels, and discarded cannons and rifles flashed through the train windows.

The rumbling of the train wheels sounded like the thunder of the far off cannons Sam heard three years earlier. A shudder went though his body. He thought he smelled gun powder. Sam pulled down the shade so as not to see, not to remember. Then he squeezed the latches on each side of the window. The window dropped suddenly. *Bam.* Sam slid out of his seat and dropped to the floor, covering his ears. *Was that gunfire?* Sam was so tired and scared. But he held it all inside—trying to act like an older brother was supposed to act. He hadn't been able to get much sleep in the four days and nights he and his family had been traveling from Canada back to their home in Georgia. They had left under General Sherman's orders when Sam was only 8-years-old. Now he was almost 12-years-old.

Scenes outside the train window got worse as they

approached their former home. The train slowed and stopped.

"We're here!"

John and George, two of Sam's younger brothers, leapt up out of their seats and ran to the end of their passenger car. The conductor held out his arms and stopped them.

"Go back to your seats, boys. Train just stopped to wait for broken tracks up ahead to be repaired.

"We'll be stopped here for an hour or so," the conductor said to Sam's father. "You can take your young'uns outside, but stay close to the train. It's not safe if you go too far away."

"Sam, you go with Emily and John and stay together," Papa said. "I'll take George and Ernest with me."

Sam held tightly to his sister with one hand and John with the other. *What did the conductor mean about not being safe?* he wondered. He followed Papa who walked briskly ahead along the right side of the track toward the caboose. A small group of dark-skinned men, huddled together around a fire, looked up when they saw Sam's father. Two of the men gathered their torn blankets around their shoulders. With outstretched arms, hands holding tin pans, they called out to him.

"Can you give us some food?"

Papa shook his head. The hungry men ambled over to the conductor standing by the train steps and held out their empty pans to him.

Sam heard them plead, "Please, we's starvin'."

The conductor pointed toward the front of the

train. "Go help 'em fix those train tracks, and then we'll feed y'all something."

Sam saw three white men in faded and torn blue uniforms come around from the other side of the train. They leered at Emily. Papa stooped to pick up some stones from the railroad bed and held them in his hand. He stood tall—as tall as his six feet could go—and clutching the stones, crossed his arms across his chest.

Between his teeth he said to the three men, "Don't you dare take another step forward or I'll throw these stones!"

He turned his head and whispered to Sam, Emily, John and the younger boys, cowering behind his legs, "Children, go quickly. I think our conductor wants you back on the train."

Sam dropped Emily and John's hands and grabbed George and Ernest's hands. The five of them scurried as fast as their legs could manage back to their passenger car.

Words tumbled over each other in locomotive speed as they tried to tell their mother what they had seen.

"Read to your brothers, Sam," Mama said after listening to their descriptions of the scenes outside the train.

"Emily, you watch the little ones while I join Papa."

Sam opened the book and started to read to his siblings, who by now had gathered around him. He wished they'd stayed in Canada where he felt safe. Even while his voice read the words on the page, his mind wandered back to that day three years earlier when they'd all been herded by Union soldiers into a freight car with their belongings.

Mama and Papa returned when the conductor called, "All aboard!"

As the train picked up speed, Sam fell asleep with the book on his lap and the bad memories came rushing back.

Flashes of lights then darkness. Train wheels clackity-clacking. Ernest and John crying. Cannons booming. Couldn't stop my body from shaking. Still heard the shots even with my hands covering my ears. Felt Papa pushing me down onto the floor...down...down. A scream bubbled up in my throat Felt Papa's big hand over my mouth. Heard Mama singing softly

> "Go to sleepy, little baby.
>
> Go to sleepy, little baby.
>
> When you wake, you'll eat a sweet cake
>
> and ride a pretty little pony.
>
> Go to sleepy..."

Wanted to throw up.

"Sam! Sam!" Papa's call woke him up. "Children, get your valises[1] ready. We're almost there." Sam stretched and shook the kink out of his neck as the train jerked and slowed. The bile was no longer in his stomach.

"S'pose we'll see Albert and Will?" Sam asked Papa. Albert and Will had been his special friends before they'd had to leave Marietta for Canada so suddenly. He'd grown up playing with both of them.

"There's one of them now," Papa said, pointing out the window as the train jerked to a stop by the station platform.

Sam tucked his scattered belongings into his rucksack[2] and took his valise from the overhead netting. He put his cap on top of his curly brown hair, grabbed his jacket, and joined the rest of his family who were peering around the conductor as he lowered the steps and placed a stool at the bottom.

ALBERT REMEMBERS

"I sees 'em," Albert said over the noise of the big engine snorting and spouting steam. He took long strides toward the Benedict family descending the train steps.

Albert wore Sam's old pants. Sam had left them in his armoire that day two and a half years before, when he'd had to leave so suddenly. A rope held the trousers around Albert's thin waist. They were too short and had been patched many times.

Albert had been testing his freedom wings since General Sherman and his soldiers had marched through Marietta. He felt like flying off with the Union soldiers. But instead he stayed in his comfortable nest in the abandoned Benedict house in Marietta. He even got to sleep in a room of his own in the big house after Sam and his family left. Albert and his family ate all the food that was left in the cellar. But when Sherman's soldiers continued on their march to Savannah, they took all the livestock with them then set fire to the house. Albert helped his father put out the fire, but not until after half the house had burned.

Then, Albert and his family moved back to their cramped cabin.

When Albert spotted Sam coming down the train steps, he shouted over the noise of the steam coming from the train's engine, "Massa Sam!"

Just then Sylvia, his mother, exclaimed, "Lawd's me, dey's got dem a new baby!" She stepped in between Albert and Sam, reaching out her arms to take the crying baby from Sam's mother.

"We're so tired, but glad to be home," Sam's mother said after she settled baby Lucy into Sylvia's welcoming arms. Sylvia cuddled Lucy, who stopped crying. She then nodded toward the half-burned house across the railroad tracks.

Albert looked back and forth between the house and Sam's mother, shielding her eyes with her gloved hands and looking in the direction of their house.

She sighed, "Oh dear, now where will we live?"

"The Kennesaw House's got dem rooms up on the second floor left," Moses, Albert's father, said. "Don't nobody wants to go up there where dem Yankees slept."

Sam's mother said, "Let's go children, grab your valises and follow the porter."

But Sam stayed back with Albert. Albert waited politely for Sam to begin the conversation, since it was customary for white masters to start conversations with slaves. Then he remembered all the old rules had changed. He didn't want to wait any longer to catch Sam up on all the news.

"We's stayin' in de cabin behind de big house,

only we's takin' folks in now. We's a bit crowded. Mattie and I has to sleep in hammocks from de rafters. Soldiers done set fire to most de whole town after y'all left—smoke everywhere. Dey used y'all's fence for firewood, too. School buildin's burnt clear to de ground. But I rescu'd some of dem books y'all left. Bin readin' reg'lar. Dey's buildin' a new school for white folks. Dey's talkin' 'bout the Freedmen findin' a buildin' for a school for us colored folk."

Albert hadn't understood why he couldn't go to school with Sam before the Great War. He had pestered his father, but Moses just shook his head and said, "Massa needs yuh to pick dis here cotton, son."

Albert remembered following Moses in the fields, pulling the cotton from the plants and filling up his bag.

I stopped picking and said, "But I wants to read too."

Someone in another row said, "'Dat's de Law. Us coloreds ain't allowed."

So I just watched Sam walk off to school and ran to greet him when he came home. Sometimes when Sam and I were alone, Sam let me look at his books and taught me some of de words .

"Have you seen, Will?" Sam's voice broke through Albert's thoughts.

Albert's face fell. " Once. He done spat in my face. He ain't my friend no mo'."

By now the porter had unloaded all of Sam's family's baggage while the rest of the family had disappeared into the Kennesaw House; however, Sam's mother turned and Albert saw her give Sam that better-obey-me look. Albert knew that look. He'd seen it many times in the big house.

When Sam picked up his valise and left to catch up with his family, Albert turned to head back toward the cabin, but Sam's hand held him back.

"Stay," Sam whispered. "Do you still have our old baseball?" he asked.

Albert nodded and the ends of his mouth turned up. When he smiled his teeth shone white against his brown skin. He had played *Around Town*[3] with the tightly wound string ball with a Drake figure eight cover. Sam, Will, Sam's brothers and sister, Emily, and his sister, Mattie, made up their teams. Instead of a regular bat, Albert chopped off a thick branch from a tree and used that for a baseball bat.

"Remember our rules?" Sam asked Albert.

"Sure I remembers. De person who hits de ball has to run 'round de fence. Den whoever done caught de ball has to touch it to de runner fer de runner to be out.

"'Member when dat war started, yer mama didn' want us playin' outside no mo'. We sometimes gits too noisy. I remembers when we played soldiers—sticks pointing at each other, sayin', 'Got yuh. You's dead.' Den we saw real soldiers..."

"Sam-u-e-l!"

Albert smiled and linked his arm with Sam's and the two boys headed for the Kennesaw House. *Just like de ole times,* Albert thought. He hadn't had many other friends besides Sam and Will. Sam had left and Albert thought he'd never see him again. Will started calling him "nigger" and the other slave kids called him "whitie" because he had always played with white kids. But Albert didn't enter the Kennesaw House. He wasn't allowed. Instead he turned and headed back to join Moses and Mattie, who were still standing on the station platform.

SAM REMEMBERS

Sam caught up with the rest of his siblings while Papa was showing them the room they would be sharing.

"Oh, there you are, Sam. Cleve and Lucy are next door. Sylvia's helping them unpack. Emily's down the hall."

Sam wished he could have his own room like Emily. Instead, he had to sleep with his noisy brothers.

Papa said, "Unpack your valises and put them under your beds. As soon as you boys are unpacked, I'll show you the room where General Sherman kept me locked up after he arrested me."

Sam had never been inside the room, so he hurried to unpack, then helped his brothers unpack. With Emily, Sam and his brothers soon joined Papa who was waiting for them at the door to the jail room.

When Papa opened the door, Sam could see that it was filled with cots.

"There weren't any cots when the Union soldiers brought me here—just a dirty mat on the floor. I didn't have any blankets—had to sleep in my vestments and cope[4]."

Sam's memories of that day's events came flooding back.

The Union soldiers stood up in the middle of a church service and demanded Papa change that prayer. I didn't understand what prayer they were talking about until Papa showed it to me later on our train ride to Canada. It was a prayer for the President and the United States Congress we had said in church every Sunday as far back as I could remember—only Papa had crossed out some words in his prayer book and substituted others so that it read:

"Most heartily we beseech thee with thy favor to behold and bless thy servant, the Governor of the Confederate States, Jefferson Davis and the Congress of the Confederate States..."

When the Union officers yelled at Papa, Papa answered, "Please sit down. You're disrupting the service."

Papa continued reading the prayer. All the people joined him. That made those officers really mad. They did sit down when Papa asked them, but as soon as the service was over, blue-coated officers from both sides of the aisle stepped out of their pews and surrounded Papa.

"Come with us," they commanded. "You're under arrest."

I sat frozen in my seat. But Mama stood up and started after the officers who held Papa, trying to pull them away. Another officer grabbed Mama's arm and led her back to our pew. She told us later the union officers

for more information or to place an order, contact:

TATE PUBLISHING & *Enterprises*

www.tatepublishing.com/bookstore
888.361.9473

Now Available

written by Terry Webb

COSTLY FREEDOM

AuthorTerryWebb.com

had taken Papa to the third floor room in the Kennesaw House and locked the door. Mama wanted to bring Papa food and clothes, but the soldiers wouldn't let her.

"Sherman's officers slept in the floor below us," Papa was saying.

Mama baked bread every day. She gave me a basket with the bread and some other food. I got Will to help me. We climbed up on top of some boxes while the soldiers outside weren't looking and managed to get a rope up to Papa. Each day that Papa was in prison, Will and I came in Will's pony cart carrying the basket of food Mama had prepared. When the soldiers went around to the other side of the building, Papa let down the rope. I jumped out of the cart with the basket, and tied it to the rope. Then Papa hauled it up. Will took the cart out into the street where he could see the soldiers on guard. Will carried a whip with him. When he held the whip up high over his shoulder, it was safe for Papa to lower the rope and get the basket. Papa also threw down folded pieces of paper with messages on them for Mama.

But when Will held the whip down low toward the ground, it meant, "Be careful, watch out, the guards are coming. Don't lower the rope." At those times I walked slowly back to the cart. If Papa had the basket in his room, it stayed there. I had to come back for it later. When I brought back the basket, I walked down the street, swing-

ing it and whistling. My insides churned and I held my breath, hoping that the soldiers wouldn't see my knees shaking and suspect something.

In one of Papa's notes, he told Mama that the Union officers had asked him once again to take out Jefferson Davis' name from that prayer and change it back to Abraham Lincoln, the President of the United States. But Papa refused.

"Gosh, Papa, weren't you scared?" John asked as we left the room.

"Sometimes, son," Papa answered. "But I prayed a lot."

"But Papa," Sam stated, "you've taught us to obey. How come you didn't change the words of that prayer when they asked you to?"

Papa thought for a long time, put his big hands on Sam's shoulders, and looked directly into his eyes and said, "Sometimes, son, we have to do what we think is right, especially when we don't respect or honor the person who tells us what to do. General Sherman and his soldiers burned their way through Georgia, took our food, killed our men, and destroyed our people's pride. They even took over our parlor at home. I had to stand up to them."

WILL REMEMBERS

The first Sunday after the Benedicts returned to Marietta, Will saw Sam sitting in the pew across the aisle from him during the church service. Will wasn't so sure he wanted to renew their friendship. So much had happened since the Great War. Sam and his family were still northerners and "northerners were never to be trusted" his father had told him. "They're all damn Yankees, especially that President Lincoln and his butcher, General Grant. Now the new president, Johnson, he was a friend to the South."

Will's thoughts wandered back to the days when he and Sam had waved goodbye to his brother, Henry, dressed in his new gray coat with blue trim.

With knapsacks on their backs, canteens jangling from their belts, and guns at the ready, Henry and the other boys going off to war turned and saluted. Sam and Will had waved their confederate flags and cheered as the eager young soldiers boarded the train pulled by the General's engine. He remembered the scene as if it were yesterday.

I thought Henry looked grand in his brand new gray uniform and forage cap[5]. I asked Papa that evening if he could get me a cap like Henry's. Papa tousled my hair, laughing. He said that the cap would be too big for me; besides he was thinking that maybe he should have one of those caps first. Mama and Papa talked and argued that night after I was supposed to be asleep. Mama said she didn't want Papa to go off to war and leave her with the farm to run. But Papa did get one of those caps. I stood beside Mama and waved my flag when he boarded the train to join the Cobb County regiment. I was proud my last name was Cobb and that Papa was off to fight for our family honor.

Sam's father's words broke through Will's thoughts. "I'm glad to be back with you," he said. Will sat there just like everyone else and stared, not caring if he had come back or not.

Will walked out of the church behind his mother. He heard Sam call, "Hey, Will. I'm back. Don't you remember me?"

"Sure. Glad you're back," Will responded, his head lowered so he wouldn't have to look over at Sam.

Sam caught up with Will and walked along beside him, but Will still didn't speak.

"Where's your father?" Sam asked. "I saw you with just your mother in church."

"Home," Will answered. He walked on with Sam beside him for what seemed like hours without saying anything else. Will looked straight ahead wishing Sam would just disappear. Will really didn't want Sam to come into his house. He didn't want anyone else to have to hear his father's tirades and constant swearing. Besides his father was usually drunk and that embarrassed him.

Finally Sam broke the silence, "Is he … ?"

"You really don't want to see him," Will said. "He just sits and stares out the window. His head is still bandaged and he lost an arm. Sometimes he's crazy mad. He swears all the time at the slaves, who've taken over our house and the farm. Mama and I have to live in one room with Papa shouting, 'those damn Yankees' or 'those good-for-nothing niggers.'"

Will kicked at a stone in the path in front of them.

"But…" Sam said slowly, quietly, "slaves—have been—freed."

"Yeah?" Will sneered. "So you've become one of those carpetbaggers,[6] too."

Besides, Will thought, *I can't let Sam see how poor we are now.* His stomach growled, but Will knew that the only food left in the house was a few yams and some corn they had hidden from Sherman's army looters. Even the money from the sale of the family silver was long since gone. *Someone is going to have to pay for what they did to us,* he thought as he clenched his fists. Fortunately his brother, Henry, had left his clothes behind when he'd gone off to fight the Yankees. Mama said that Will could wear some of them. They certainly couldn't afford new ones.

Will still missed his brother, Henry. But Sam? Will wasn't sure they could ever be friends again. He turned around to see if Sam was still there walking beside him, but instead he saw him heading back the other direction. *Just as well,* Will thought as he opened the door to his house and heard Papa's raving.

SAM VISITS

Will's attitude puzzled Sam. He'd been so excited to see his former friend. But it was obvious that Will didn't really want to have much to do with him. Besides Sam wasn't sure what Will meant when he'd called him a carpetbagger.

"Are we carpetbaggers?" Sam asked.

Mama looked over at Papa seated at the head of the table. Sam waited for Papa to answer.

"No, but we've just arrived from the North. Anyone coming from the North is suspicious. That's probably why the congregation didn't respond when I told them I was glad to be back."

Papa went on talking as if just he and Mama were seated at the table to listen to each other, but Sam listened too.

"I guess the members of the church are still numb from the war since so much of the town is burned, and their whole way of life was pulled out from under them. It will be a difficult time for all of us." Mama nodded. Papa went back to eating.

Sam wanted to share about his disappointments too since he'd been back in Georgia. Instead, he gulped back a sob, almost choking on a mouthful of food. Everything was different here—not like it was before. Sam wished they were back in Canada, especially this time of year when snow sledding and sleigh riding made the cold winters such fun. Here in Georgia the land was brown and broken—people too.

"I thought I should go visiting after dinner," Papa said to Mama.

"Can we come, too?" John asked.

Papa smiled. "Well how about just Sam and you, no one else. You both can walk with me to Albert's cabin. I'll leave you there with Albert's family, and then go on to visit some of the members of our parish."

I really don't want John tagging along, Sam thought. *But if I object, Papa probably won't let me go either.* So Sam kept his mouth shut. They had to wear their coats, because even though they were away from the snowy north, February winds still chilled the air.

They crossed to the other side of the railroad tracks and started walking toward their old house. As they walked they stepped around and sometimes between groups of men.

"Help me," one white man said, crawling over to Papa and holding up a tin cup. Some dark-skinned men with stubby beards and ragged clothes beckoned to them as they passed.

"Where y'all goin' with them young'uns?"

The men staggered over to the three of them wagging their fingers and shouting. Papa grabbed Sam and

John, holding them tightly by their hands and walking faster. The two boys had to trot to keep up with his long strides. Sam heard the men behind them jeering and cussing. He held tightly to his father's big hand—glad that he could stand up to such men—until they finally reached their old house.

Groups of dark-skinned men were camped out all around the field and what was left of the lawn. Some were singing spirituals. When the men noted the arrival of the white folks, many of them rushed over and surrounded the three of them. Sam and John waited while Papa listened to their pleas for work and for food.

"We's good field hands."

"Can we help yuh rebuild dis house?"

"Have any food to spare? My baby, she's 'bout starvin' to death."

Papa nodded and pulled Sam and John closer to his side.

"Now folks, make way." Moses' voice carried above the din of demands.

The crowd parted and Moses led the Benedicts into his cabin and offered Papa the only chair in their family's cramped living quarters. Sam nodded to Albert who just grinned back.

"Will the boys be safe with you while I visit some folks in our congregation?" Papa asked Sylvia.

"Sure 'nough, Massa Benedict," she said. When Papa left, John stayed in the cabin to play with Mattie while Sam sat with Albert outside on their stoop to talk.

Terry Webb

ALBERT AND FREEDOM

"What's it like?" Sam asked Albert. "Being emancipated?"

"What yuh mean?"

"I mean, what you said about being free," Sam said.

Albert grinned, stood up, and thumped his chest. "See...I's me. I's a person...Can't nobody own me..., can't nobody boss me, 'cept my Mammy and Pappy...can be who I wants to be when I's grow'd up."

"What do you want to be?" Sam asked.

"Don't want to be no field hand like my Pappy and all these other colored folks." Albert waved his hand from one side of the cabin to the other, taking in all the darkies they could see camped around the big house. "Wants to be somebody with learnin'. Maybe learnin' others like you learn'd me."

"But you can't go to school," Sam said.

Albert's face lit up and he sat back down on the stoop.

"Goin' to school secret like," he whispered. "Some of us…" He looked around. "De Freedmen—dey's teachin' us."

Albert remembered when he had joined a throng of former slave children surrounding the tall soldier in his blue uniform with the brass buttons. The soldier sat high upon his horse and exclaimed, "Soon you will have your school." Albert had gone to sleep that night with hope in his heart and these thoughts in his head.

I don't want to go back to yesterday. No siree. When de slave traders took Mammy away, I held tight to Mattie's chubby hand. Den dem bad mens snatched Mattie away from Mammy and dragged Mammy to dat auction block. Den Massa Sam done bought her. He boughts Pappy too. But we chillens were put back in de holdin' pen for 'nother day's sale. We was so scared, but Pappy done makes me promise to be de big boy and take good care of Mattie, so I helds onto her tight all night with her sobbin' 'gainst my chest. Didn' rightly knows what would become of us. Next day Massa Sam comes back with Mammy and Pappy. Sure 'nough don't he up and buys us too, so's we could be a family agin. Dat's hows Sam and I gots to be friends.

"And here I is—e-man-si-pated. Can't nobody sell me no mo'."

Albert stood up and stuck his thumbs under his armpits and puffed out his thin chest. Albert pulled

Sam up to stand beside him, took one of his arms and held it up high with his.

He proudly proclaimed, "See's we's equals now!"

He sat back down on the steps again with his old friend and continued, "Dem Freedmens gave Pappy forty acres of land to farm. Gots us a mule too. I's been helpin' 'im with plantin' and harvestin'. Only we's got to ride a long way to gits to it and de harvest weren't too good dis year."

There was a long pause as Albert waited for Sam to say something.

"Brought some marbles, want to play?" Sam asked. He took out a cloth bag tied with a string. Albert drew a ten-inch circle in the red soil with a stick. Sam counted out twelve marbles and placed them in the shape of a cross inside the circle. He gave the shooter to Albert.

"You start. We'll play *Friendlies*."

Albert got off the stoop and carefully eyed for the best angle to shoot.

The two of them took turns playing until other boys sauntered over one by one to watch. Eventually Sam asked them to join in the play.

After they'd been playing awhile, one of the older boys the others called Abe said, "Dem Yankees taught us'uns *Ole Bowler*. Said Pres'dent Lincoln liked dis game de best. My Mammy done renamed me after 'im."

Abe drew a large square in the dirt with a stick and put a marble in each corner. Then he took another marble in his hand and turned to the other boys and said, "Dis one's de Ole Bowler." He placed that marble in the middle of the square. Then he drew a straight line way back from the square.

"Dis is de taw line. Y'all gits a shot at de corner marbles behind dis here line. If yuh miss, yuh lose yer turn. If yuh hits, yuh keeps de marble yuh hit. If yer shooter hits one of dem and lands outside de circle, then yuh gits to pick it up. But if' n it lands inside, den yuh has to leave it there and use 'nother marble as a shooter. De winner collects de most marbles. De game's over when one of y'all hits de ole bowler out. But if yuh hits de ole bowler a'fore all de other marbles are hit, dat means you's out."

They were so busy playing *Old Bowler*, Albert didn't notice when their two fathers returned until Sam's father said, "Think it's time we were heading back, Sam." The other boys looked up at the big, tall man with the bushy black-white beard, pushed the marbles they had collected back toward Sam, and shuffled away. Albert helped Sam put the marbles back in the bag and gave it to Sam, who then slung it over his shoulder.

Albert fixed his eyes on the shadows that trailed beside Sam, John, and Reverend Benedict as they crossed over the railroad tracks. He rose from the step where he was sitting, took off his faded and worn cap, and rubbed his curly closely shaven black hair.

WILL WATCHES

After he returned from the church service, Will asked his mother what they were going to eat for Sunday dinner. She shook her head and shrugged her shoulders.

"I'll find something," she replied and went off to beg from one of their former slaves now occupying the first floor rooms of the house.

After his father's earlier outburst, Will was glad for the relative quiet. Papa was now sitting staring out the window. His false teeth were on the table and he was stroking his bald head with his only hand.

Will's stomach was still growling when he heard footsteps coming up onto the front porch.

"Why Reverend Benedict," Will heard Mama say, "how nice of you to come calling. I'd ask you in but we have no chairs downstairs here to sit upon."

Will leaned over the banister. There was Sam's father and Moses standing in the front parlor, hats in hand. Some cinnamon-brown faces peeked out from the parlor. Moses beckoned to the one they called Jeremiah, their old butler. Jeremiah spoke to one of the others in such a low voice, Will couldn't understand what he said until two others brought out three chairs. Will watched as Mama spread out her outer skirt over her hoop, took up the fan hooked to her waist and started fanning herself. Will guessed she was uncomfortable thinking that Moses might sit down in one of the chairs, but Moses left the hall and headed for the kitchen. Will's mother finally sat down.

Sam's father cleared his throat and said, "I'm just making my rounds of parishioners and wanted to come and visit with you first. Your husband was one of our elders. How is he, by the way? I missed seeing him in church."

There was a long silence. Will listened as his mother replied, "He's home from the war. Lost an arm."

Just then Will's father screamed, "Those damn Yankees!"

Reverend Benedict turned his head and looked up toward the direction of where the scream had come.

"He's like that now." Will's mother stopped fanning and looked down at her lap. Will listened but couldn't hear the rest of her words. He leaned his head in between the banister railings.

"When the surgeon amputated his arm, he gave him blue pills[7] for the pain. But they don't seem to help."

Reverend Benedict cleared his throat again. "And how are you?"

Will wanted to shout out. *We're awful! And I'm always hungry!*

But Mama just shook her head and dabbed at her eyes with her handkerchief.

Will watched and listened from his observation place at the top of the stairs for his mother to answer. He'd closed the door so his Papa's screams were now muffled.

"I don't know what we're going to do," she said between sobs. Will watched as her tears fell onto her lap. "Our field hands have left and the Yankees burned the cotton bales; our confederate money is worthless and..." she paused and blew her nose. She looked up at Will staring through the banister railings and finished, "...we're hungry all the time."

Will's stomach growled. He saw Reverend Benedict open and then close his prayer book and lean over to place his big arm around Mama's shoulders and say, "I came back to town so I could help you." He paused and then added, "Are any of your house servants still here?"

Moses reappeared from the kitchen with two plates in his hands. "Cook said they's made some patties from the last of the corn and 'tators in the cellar."

Will's mouth watered.

"Here's one fer Miss Cobb and t'other's for Massa Will 'bout ready to fall off that there balcony."

Reverend Benedict laughed. "Here, I'll take it up to him then look in on Hank Cobb."

He started up the winding staircase but Will had already begun to descend, his hand outstretched while trying to ignore the cries coming from the closed doors behind him. He met Reverend Benedict half way down the stairs, took the plate, sat down on a step and gobbled up all the food on the plate. He didn't even notice when Reverend Benedict reached the landing on the top of the winding stairs, opened the door, and slipped inside.

SAM REMEMBERS

"Papa," John asked as he and Sam walked back from Moses' cabin to the Kennesaw House, "did you visit any of my friends?"

"Do you remember Will Cobb?" Papa asked. John nodded his head.

Sam answered, "He's my friend."

"Well, I took him a plate of food and I visited with his mama and papa."

"Will told me Mr. Cobb lost his arm in the war," Sam said.

"Many men did, son. Legs, too."

Sam looked through the window at the men hobbling along without a leg or an arm. Then he remembered seeing that pile of cut off limbs at the back door of St. James Church when he'd gone with Papa to visit the wounded soldiers being treated there. Memories and sights and smells came flooding back.

We passed a gray pile with a hand sticking out as we entered the church. I held onto Papa's hand more tightly. Papa gave me his handkerchief. The smell was horrible and made me feel sick, so I put the handkerchief over my nose. Groans and screams came from the men lying on mats or cots scattered all over the church floor where the pews used to be.

Papa walked around and looked at all the names posted on the foot of each cot, and stopped when he came to a cot with the name, Henry. His head was bandaged. Henry tossed and turned on his cot. His hair was gone and his eyes were sort of glazed over. Papa leaned over him and said a prayer. Henry's lips moved. I heard nearby groans and glanced over at the cot next to Henry's as two men lifted that man onto a stretcher and placed a block of wood in his mouth.

"Bite on this," they told him, "until we put you out."

While Papa was praying over Henry, I watched the men carrying the stretcher weave it between the beds to a table at the front of the church where the altar used to be—or was it still the altar? I wasn't sure. A man in a dirty apron put a funnel over the wounded man's mouth and dropped some liquid from three different bottles into the funnel. I pulled on the edge of Papa's frock coat. "What are they doing?" I whispered.

"They're getting ready to amputate his leg. That's the surgeon," Papa said, pointing to the man with the dirty apron standing by the table with a saw. As soon as the wounded man went limp, the surgeon started sawing on his leg and blood came spurting out everywhere. Now I

knew I would be sick. I gagged and tugged frantically on Papa's coat, pointing toward the door. Before we'd gotten to the door, my meal all came up. Papa just took back his handkerchief, grabbed a nearby mop, and cleaned up the mess. Then he took me home.

The old queasy feeling came back and Sam put his hand over his mouth. Papa must have remembered too, because he said, "You're okay now, son. Now tell me about your time with Albert."

Even while Sam was telling him about Albert, he was thinking about Will. The Henry that Papa had come to visit at the makeshift church hospital died that same night. He was Will's brother.

"How was Will?" he asked his father. "Was he okay?"

"I'm not sure 'okay' is the right word for Will, but I know he was hungry the way he gobbled up that plate of food." Papa chuckled and continued, "But his father wasn't okay. I'd say he was—well—mad in the head."

"That's what Will told me."

"Too bad," Papa sighed. "He used to be a pretty smart businessman."

Sam thought back to the days when he'd visited Will and had seen Mr. Cobb at his desk with his ledger books all around him giving orders to the slaves on his farm. If that was what war did to someone like him, Sam knew he didn't ever want to be a soldier.

SAM AND EMILY

"First thing we need to do is find a way to get food to folks," Papa announced to Mama at supper that night.

"Albert told me the harvest was bad this fall," Sam added.

"What about the Ladies Gunboat Association?" Mama suggested. "They raised enough money raffling those quilts here in Georgia to purchase a gunboat for the Confederate Army. Maybe they could raffle those same quilts to raise money for food."

Sam thought about the many times he'd seen the same quilt raffled over again and again when Will's mama and others conducted their raffles. He wondered if that quilt was still around.

"Not sure anyone around here has enough money to even bid on a quilt." Papa sighed.

"But we're eating," Emily said.

"So we are, daughter," Papa replied. "Maybe our cook knows where and how we can keep folks around here from starving to death this winter."

Sam and Emily went with Papa to talk to the cook

in the Kennesaw House kitchen after supper. She told them that most of the food for the freed colored folk was brought in by the Freedmen's Bureau and supplied by northern churches.

"And how does one get this food?" Papa asked.

The cook just shrugged her shoulders.

"My man, he done brung it from one of de wagons when dey comes through town. Once a week de train drops food bundles. Just goes to where 'tis at and grabs—'bout all."

Sam looked over at Emily. He remembered when he and Will brought food to Papa when he was on the top floor of this same Kennesaw House and the light bulb went off in his head.

"Papa?" He asked, "Can we go to Will's house again tomorrow?"

His father scowled and replied, "We're talking about finding a way to keep folks from starving and you want to go play."

"Please Papa. I have an idea," Sam pleaded.

Papa shrugged his shoulders and turned back to the cook. "Got any extra food you can spare to take to some hungry parishioners?" he asked.

"Wagon's due in tomorrow. Go grab some yo'self. But best wear that black suit with the white collar—yuh ain't got dark skin."

Sam saw Papa's shocked reaction to cook's sullen tone of voice. "Maybe Moses will come with me," he mumbled.

"We'll come," Sam and Emily said in unison.

"No," Papa answered. "Too dangerous."

"But you'll need us to help carry the food," Emily argued.

But Papa wasn't convinced. After supper he walked alone across the railroad tracks to ask Moses to meet him the next morning and take him to the wagon drop off point.

That night Sam waited until his brothers were fast asleep, then he tiptoed into Emily's room.

"Are you asleep?" he whispered.

Emily sat up in bed and rubbed her eyes.

"If I was, you just woke me up. What are you doing in here? If Mama catches you, she'll tan your hide."

"Want to go watch?"

"Where?" Emily answered.

"When the wagons come in. We can stay behind Moses and Papa so they won't see us."

Emily sat up in bed, put her hands on her chin and looked at Sam.

"Why?"

"'Cause of my idea."

"What idea?"

"You'll see. First we need to find out where the wagons drop off the food."

Early the next morning, Papa, dressed in his black preacher clothes, started off with Moses. They both carried empty boxes and bags. Sam and Emily followed them, darting behind buildings and trees hoping they couldn't be seen.

"Look," whispered Emily, "see the wagons are coming."

Sam's eyes focused on the place where her hand pointed and saw the dust rising and heard the rumbling of the wagon wheels. Figures from all directions carrying baskets and crocus sacks[8] converged on the two wagons with their hands outstretched. Sam could just make out Moses and Papa approach one of the wagons, holding out their baskets and sacks. A woman in one of the wagons filled them and motioned the two men to move back through the crowd.

"Wonder what they got?" Sam whispered.

"Let's head back to the Kennesaw House before they spot us."

A big stocky ebony-colored man stepped in front of them as Sam and Emily tried to retrace their steps. "What you white chillens doin' out here?" he asked. Sam turned to look behind him to two figures, who looked like Papa and Moses, coming closer,

Sam said, "Please let us by. We were just out for a walk before breakfast."

Emily just nodded, but reached over for Sam's hand.

"And Mama will be worried if we don't run home."

The man moved aside and Emily started running, pulling Sam along. They reached the Kennesaw House just in time to sit down at the breakfast table as Papa and Moses came through the door. Papa was saying to Moses, "Soon as breakfast is over we'll take these out to the Cobb farm."

Sam jumped up out of his chair and the chair fell clattering to the floor.

"Pick it up, Sam," his mother scolded. "And don't be in such a rush. Papa hasn't even had a chance to eat his breakfast."

Moses headed for the kitchen while Papa ate his porridge.

"What kind of food did you bring back?" Emily asked.

Papa nodded to the sacks and baskets he and Moses had left by the door.

"You can look, but don't taste. They're for the Cobbs."

Sam joined Emily, who was examining the contents of the baskets and sacks. In them were peanuts, potatoes, some bread, a ham, and some greens. And after the others had finished their breakfast, both Sam and Emily joined Papa and Moses to carry the food to Moses' wagon to take to the Cobb farm. Then Sam climbed in beside Papa and they were on their way.

SAM AND HIS IDEA

As their wagon drove up the circular driveway, Sam stared at the stately white columns—now turning gray with peeling paint—the overgrown lawn and the once flourishing gardens choked with weeds. He remembered the Cobb farm before the war, majestically standing amidst stately rows of shade trees. These, too, were now sparse and bare.

Then he saw Will sitting on what was left of the front steps with his elbows on his knees and his head cupped on his hands. Will gave the wagon a blank stare when it pulled in front of the house and Moses called out "whoa boy" to the mule while pulling the reins taut.

Sam jumped off the wagon first and cautiously approached Will, remembering that he hadn't been very friendly when Sam had last seen him.

"Hi," he ventured. No response came.

"Come help us unload," Papa called.

Sam turned. Moses dropped a sack at Will's feet.

"Dis here fer de kitchen," he said, picking up

another sack and handing it to Sam. Sam saw Will's head pop up when Moses said the word kitchen. He thought Will's eyes seemed brighter than usual when Sam passed by him carrying his bundle. He heard Moses say, "Dis here's for you, Will." And Will muttered, "I'm not taking any orders from no nigger."

When Sam returned from taking his sack into the kitchen, Will's sack was still at his feet.

But by the time Sam retrieved a basket of food from Moses, Will had picked up his sack and followed Sam back into the kitchen.

After they gave their sacks and baskets of food to the cook, Will grabbed a handful of peanuts from one of the sacks and followed Sam outside. The two boys sat down on the front steps, dropping peanut shells on the ground as they ate.

"Still got that tree house?" Sam asked.

"No. We used the wood from the house for fires," Will answered but said no more. Instead, he took a stick and started scratching in the dry earth.

"Remember when we took food to Papa in your pony cart when he was locked up in the Kennesaw House?" Sam asked.

"What about it?" Will answered.

"Do you still have the cart? I have an idea."

"So what...you always have ideas."

"Want to help me?"

"Help you do what? I hid the cart where those darn soldiers couldn't find it after they stole my pony and all our horses. Don't know whether it's still there," Will replied in a sullen tone of voice.

Sam stood up and pulled Will up beside him.

"Where did you hide it? Let's go find it"

"Out on the other side of the cotton fields..." Will pointed in the direction of the fields. "...in those bushes."

Sam walked with Will through the stalks of cotton with their fluffy tops. Here and there dark-skinned boys and girls were plucking off the tops and putting them in bags slung over their shoulders. Bales of cotton lay piled on either side of the field.

Will hit the stalks with his stick as they passed, knocking some of the cotton off. Will's stick made no distinction between cotton stalk and picker. The pickers stopped what they were doing and one boy called,

"Dis here's my row."

Will ignored the speaker and continued talking to Sam. "Those darn Negros say they own these fields now. Papa would have whipped their hides if they'd dared talk back before..." His voice trailed off.

They reached the end of the fields and Will used his stick to poke around the bushes until he hit something.

"Guess it's still here—right where I hid it." He motioned to Sam. "Help me pull it out."

Sam helped Will pull on the two arms of the cart, finally managing to disentangle the cart from the bushes and brambles that covered it.

"Now what do we want to do with it? Ain't no horses around here," Will snarled.

"But how many mules are around?"

Will shrugged his shoulders.

"I know Albert's family has a mule. Let's look for one and hitch her up."

"What for?"

"So we can bring you food."

"From where?"

Sam then told Will about the train and wagons bringing food collected by churches in the northern states and sent to southern states for former slaves.

"Maybe one of them could help us find a mule."

"Those good-for-nothing…" Will kicked at the wheel of the cart.

"Let's ask Moses," Sam finished his suggestion. "Com'on. Help me move this cart."

Each boy took an arm of the cart and managed to move it up beside the house. Sam's father and Moses were already in their wagon when they reached the big house.

"What yuh goin' to do wid dat?" Moses asked.

"Can you see if anyone here has a mule around that could pull it?" Sam asked.

Moses just grinned. "Looks like you two young'uns make mighty fine ole mules."

Sam ignored Moses's comment and said to his father, "Remember when Will brought you food in this cart when you were locked in that third floor room, Papa? It can carry food again if Moses can help us find a mule."

By this time a crowd of cinnamon and light brown colored faces were peering over the rim of the pony cart. Will, meanwhile, had backed away.

Ira, one of the boys spoke up with, "I knows where we gits dat mule."

Sam grabbed his arm and held up his hand. "Then you can help us."

"Dont' touch that—nigger," Will swore from the background. Sam tried to ignore Will's comment but anger rose up in his throat.

By the time Moses had taken Sam and Papa back to the Kennesaw House, Sam had told them both about his idea to take food to other farms. Papa had finally agreed to the plan as long as their former slaves could also share in the food relief. He reminded Sam that the food being shipped into Marietta was for freed slaves and was not meant for any of the outlying white farm owners.

"But they're hungry, too." Sam argued. Papa slapped him on the back. "You're right, son. We'll see if our parishioners have any other of those pony carts hidden in their bushes."

Over the next few days, Sam and his father devised their plan. When the train arrived carrying bundles of food from northern states, Will's pony cart with a mule hitched to it along with others would be on the station platform prepared to take food to outlying farms. Although Will had agreed that Ira could borrow his cart, he refused to go along to collect the food.

SAM MEETS MASTER CALHOUN

Sam watched from a Kennesaw House window later that week as Ira pulled up alongside the train in Will's pony cart. Moses and Albert were there with their wagon along with other mule-pulled carts. Sam had tried to persuade his father to allow him to join the others on the train platform, but Papa had told him those distributing food probably wouldn't give any bundle of food to a lone white boy.

"Maybe our idea is working," Sam said to Emily, who was standing beside him at the window, but it seemed to Sam that Emily was more interested in watching the ladies in their ballooning skirts stepping down from the passenger car. Swarms of brown to ebony dark-skinned former slaves gathered outside the baggage car. As the sacks and bundles of food were unloaded, the ladies helped to distribute the food as equally as possible.

"Look," Sam said to Emily, "see that tall man in a

wrinkled suit just stepping down from the train. Wonder who he is?" Tufts of red hair appeared when the man took off his hat. He walked over to the baggage car and helped the ladies with the unloading of the food. It looked to Sam as if he was saying something to every boy and girl who came forward. After loading their carts and wagons the boys and girls came back to stand around the red-headed man. As soon as the platform was empty the red-headed man picked up his valises and headed for the Kennesaw House instead of getting back on the train with the ladies.

Just then Sam heard his mother call them for breakfast, interrupting their vigil by the window. When Sam sat down at the breakfast table, he was surprised to see that the stranger they had seen talking to the boys and girls by the train was already seated at their table.

"Where do you hail from, young man?" Mama asked, "And what brings you to Marietta?"

"Name's Thomas, ma'am, Thomas Calhoun. I hail from Pennsylvania and I came south when the Methodist Missionary Society put out a call for volunteers to start schools for former slave children. I came with the rest of our missionary group bringing food supplies. Seems there's lots of interest from the freed slaves around here. Guess you need me here."

"It's not only slaves who need schooling. In this town even the former St. James School where I was principal was destroyed when Sherman's army came through," Papa said.

Thomas Calhoun winked at Sam, Emily, and

John. "So what about the children who attended your school?"

"We just got came back into town ourselves," Mama replied. "My father started a school in his home. I'd like to do that too, but our old house isn't livable."

"Perhaps I could help, ma'am," Mr. Calhoun answered. "That is if you are willing to have your children learn with the former slave boys and girls. We just need to find a building that has space to hold classes, that's all."

Mama smiled. Papa frowned.

"I'm not sure that one location for a school is such a good idea, yet," Papa said. "I think it would be better to have two school buildings, one for colored children and one for whites."

"But there aren't that many buildings left standing in this town,' Mama said. "Besides, why can't both coloreds and whites be taught together? The War's over. Slavery is dead," she added.

Sam remembered the heated conversation he had overhead between Mama and Papa when Papa bought Sylvia and Moses.

Mama had said, "Samuel Benedict, we can't afford to buy slaves." And Papa answered, "Julia, you need help taking care of Ernest, especially with another baby on the way." Then Mama stomped her foot and shouted at Papa, "I don't believe in owning slaves!"

I never heard her so mad. I thought she must be an

abolitionist[9] like Grandpa. He and Papa had argued just like Papa and Mama were doing now.

Sam was confused. He didn't often disagree with Papa, but Albert was his friend.

"I want to go to school with Albert, Papa," he said.

"The Law..." Papa began.

"Sir, that Law is null and void since the Civil Rights Act of 1866 and the Thirteenth Amendment were approved," Mr. Calhoun argued.

"But not yet here in Georgia," Papa insisted.

"Then Georgia and the rest of the Confederate states better get used to the fact that the Civil War is over. The Federal Government now makes the laws and their old rebel laws aren't any good anymore," Mr. Calhoun said hitting the table with his hand for emphasis.

"I agree with Reverend Benedict," said Mrs. Fletcher, who had just sat down at the table to join in the conversation. She turned to Mr. Calhoun. "You, young man, are too idealistic. They're just not ready here in Georgia for full integration of blacks and whites."

Sam remembered that Mrs. Louisa Fletcher and his Papa had disagreed on many issues before the War, and now she was agreeing with him. He had heard Papa say she had some strange ideas and people in the church say she had "northern sympathies." Sam didn't understand.

"What about the Superintendent's house at the

Georgia Military Institute?" Mrs. Fletcher spoke again. "That building was the only one on the grounds not burned by Sherman's soldiers. It has plenty of room for classes. I can take Mr. Calhoun out there to look over the building tomorrow to see if it might be suitable for his school."

"Thanks, ma'am," Mr. Calhoun said. "I'd appreciate that. I could sure use your help."

WILL SKIPS SCHOOL

Will's mother insisted that he come with her to the church service the next Sunday. *At least,* thought Will, *my stomach isn't growling anymore.* The service was boring so he slouched down as far as he could go without falling off the pew seat, but straightened up when a stranger walked up to the front of the church.

Reverend Benedict said, "I want you to meet our new school master, Thomas Calhoun. He has come to town with the group of Methodist missionaries who brought in food supplies last week and is starting a new school."

"Howdy, folks," Master Calhoun said. "The school will be open tomorrow at the Georgia Military Institute's Superintendent's building. Anyone wishing to enroll children please see me after the service."

As soon as the service ended, Will's mother took him by the elbow and directed him to where Master Calhoun was signing up students. Before Will could object, she had enrolled him in the school.

"But Mama," Will whined on the way home,

"Why'd you do that? I don't want to go to school. Since Papa's not well, I'm the only one who can manage the farm."

"Well, you won't be able to manage the farm without finishing your schooling. So you're going. Tomorrow!"

The next morning she rousted Will out of bed and pushed him out the door. Will shuffled along complaining to himself as he walked to the site of the former Georgia Military Institute. He found he wasn't alone on the road. Multi-colored boys and girls seemed to appear from behind every tree. *Wonder why they're not out in the fields picking cotton where they should be?* Will thought. He tried to ignore their presence. *At least I don't have to speak to them and they can't speak to me unless I speak to them first.*

Will couldn't help overhearing them singing:

I free. I free.

I free as a frog.

I free till I fool!

Glory Alleluia.[10]

I don't care how free you think you are, you're still not equal to me. But Will didn't dare say this thought out loud because there were more of them and only one of him. So he let them pass him by. *Maybe they're all going fishing. Good for nothings. Ought to get a good whipping.* Then he remembered. *Papa can't whip them. When the wagons and train bring food for the niggers, if I whip them I might not get any of that food.* He wished now he hadn't gotten talked into lending Reverend Benedict his pony cart.

Will heard the school bell ring while lost in his dark thoughts. Since he was still far away from the Georgia Military Superintendent's building, he didn't hurry to catch up. *They'll just have to wait for Will Cobb. We own the biggest farm in town after all.* Then he remembered that his family didn't own the land anymore. Their former slaves had claimed ownership of all the farming property. *But I'll get everything back for Papa and then they'll find out who is really boss.* He kicked at a stone in his path and sent it into a nearby tree.

Will climbed the steps into the school building and found Mrs. Fletcher sitting on a chair by the door with a list of names. "You're late," she said. "What's your name and your age?" Will told her and she checked his name off her list.

"First door on your right. Class roll call has started."

Will opened the door and stared. All he saw were dark-skinned faces. He backed out the same door he had entered.

"I'm not going to school with no Negros," he spouted out to Mrs. Fletcher as he brushed past her and out the building. He stooped down and scooped up some stones from the path and threw them against the building. Mrs. Fletcher came to the door with her arms folded across her chest and stared down at Will.

"See here now, Will Cobb. If you continue that behavior I'll report you to the sheriff."

"What sheriff? Yankee soldiers burned down the courthouse."

Will turned his back on Mrs. Fletcher and headed down the road toward home.

"Insolent young man," he heard Mrs. Fletcher say, but Will ignored her.

ALBERT GOES TO SCHOOL

Albert stopped loading food bundles on to their wagon when he heard the red-haired man say that he had come to town to start a school for freed slave boys and girls. He'd dropped the sacks he was carrying and ran to stand right in front of the school teacher and said.

"I's ready fer more schoolin.'"

"Come back here," Pappy Moses hollered. He had sat down on the bundles of food Albert had been loading on to the wagon so no one else could grab them.

"Better go back to your papa," Master Calhoun told him. "What's your name?" he called after him as he reluctantly returned to loading food supplies.

"Albert!" he called back.

Now he was seated in the classroom and waiting proudly for the new schoolteacher to call his name. They were all of them waiting for Master Calhoun to call roll.

"Albert?" Master Calhoun called out. "What's your last name?"

Albert hesitated. He'd never heard Pappy say his last name. When he'd asked Pappy about their family name, Pappy just said, "Don't rightly knows 'cause we's owned by Benedicts."

"Benedict..." he said. It was more of a question than an answer.

Sam, who was sitting two rows behind, said, "Mine, too."

Master Calhoun looked from one to the other. His brow creased and then relaxed as a smile came over his face. "Any more Benedict kin in this class?"

Emily and John raised their hands. So did Mattie.

When Master Calhoun reached the end of roll call, he divided the boys and girls into age groups and gave each child a slate.

"Now write your name on your slate," he said.

Albert looked back at Sam and proudly wrote his name on the slate. Sam had taught him that much, but he knew Mattie couldn't write hers. In fact, most of the other former slave children couldn't either.

Their new schoolteacher divided them up again—those who couldn't write their names were put in one group and those who could in another. Albert, Sam, Emily, and John were each given a primer to read. Master Calhoun asked Mrs. Fletcher to listen to Albert's group read. Meanwhile he wrote and pronounced the alphabet letters on the black chalkboard in front of the classroom for the others to copy on their slates.

Albert was just about to get a turn to read from his primer when Master Calhoun dismissed the class. He didn't even have a chance to learn anything new. After he had gathered up his slate and put on his jacket, another group of boys and girls were standing in the yard waiting for their turn. Then he remembered that Mrs. Fletcher announced that morning that there were so many children registered they would have to hold separate but equal classes of pupils—one in the morning, one in the afternoon, and one in the evening for adults. Even Pappy had registered for the adult evening class. *Seems like de 'hole town wants schoolin,'* Albert thought.

SAM, EMILY, AND JOHN

"How was school?" Papa asked Sam, Emily and John at dinner that night.

"We're all in the same group," Sam answered.

"Will didn't stay...," Emily said, "...in the classroom. But he must have hung around because on the way home he threw rocks at some of the colored kids."

"One boy got hit on his leg," John added.

"I wrapped my shawl around it," Emily added.

Papa frowned and said to Emily, "I'm glad you helped him but I think I better walk with you to school tomorrow."

The next day when Papa walked Sam, Emily, and John to school, they saw Will with some older white kids. They all had mean looks on their faces. The boys had stones in their fists and were getting ready to throw them until they saw Papa.

"Will, put down those stones and go to school," Papa demanded in a stern voice.

"Just make us, nigger lover," one of the older boys

jeered. Then Will and the other boys disappeared behind some trees and Sam, Emily, and John went safely inside. After Sam's father turned around and headed back down the path, the boys started pelting the building with stones.

Master Calhoun came outside to tell them to stop. Inside the building dark and white faces peered out the windows. Sam gasped with horror as he watched Will pick up a rock and throw it directly at Master Calhoun. The rock hit him on the forehead. He stumbled back, then collapsed at the bottom of the steps. Mrs. Fletcher came rushing out the door and down the steps. She pressed her handkerchief against the school master's wound to stop the bleeding. "Do you hurt anywhere else?" she asked as he tried moving his arms and legs.

"I don't think so, but I'm seeing stars."

Sam could see a lump starting on his forehead.

"I'm not in any condition to teach. Please dismiss the students for the day."

Sam and Emily, with John in tow, walked Master Calhoun back to town and they took him to Mrs. Fletcher's house where he had leased a room. Mrs. Fletcher called Sam's mother to come over to look at the head wound. Emily held a cold cloth on their schoolteacher's forehead and Sam read to him, while John squeezed his hand because Mama said,

"Keep him awake to make sure he hasn't had a concussion."

That afternoon Mrs. Fletcher came over to the Kennesaw House and asked to see Papa. Together they wrote the following notice:

Due to some recent violence against our students and their teacher, school will be discontinued until after a town meeting tomorrow night at 7 PM to discuss a safety plan for students, their teacher and helpers.

Papa asked Sam and Emily to copy the message, then take the copies and post them on the door of the Kennesaw House, the school door, and around town. All evening and into the next day, Sam watched people line up outside the Kennesaw House to read the message. Colored folk knocked on the door to inquire about Master Calhoun. White folk insisted on coming inside to talk to Papa.

"They'll be a heap more trouble if you let that Carpetbagger permit those Negros to be in the same room with our children!" Sam overheard one white man scream at Papa.

Sam didn't really want to tell anyone that he'd seen his old friend Will throw the rock that hurt Master Calhoun. Yet, he knew that what Will had done was bad and that he might do more mean things like that if he stayed so bitter. The three of them—Albert, Will and Sam—had been such close friends before the Great War. Now, Will didn't want to be in the same room with Albert. *Maybe if I talk to Will,* Sam thought. So he decided that the next day, when there weren't any classes, he would visit Will and try and talk some sense into him before he got into any more trouble.

SAM MEETS WILL

So the next day Moses drove Sam to Will's house. When Sam asked Mrs. Cobb to see Will, she said, "Thought you'd be in school. That's where Will said he was heading."

"School's cancelled today. There's a meeting tonight," Sam answered while in his head he thought, *And if I told you that your son, Will, had thrown a rock at the school teacher yesterday and hurt him, Will would get a whipping from his papa.* Then Sam remembered that Will's father probably couldn't understand.

"Some older boys stopped by earlier," Mrs. Cobb said, interrupting Sam's secret thought. "Will said he was walking to school with them. Hope he's not in some kind of trouble. I'll ask Jeremiah if he knows whether he came back."

"Mind if I look for him around here?" Sam asked. "I think I know where he might be."

"Go ahead. Hope you find him," Will's mother replied.

Sam took off across the cotton field to look first

where he and Will had built their tree house and Will had hidden the pony cart. When he reached the clearing and the bushes near the large oak tree where the cart had been hidden, he didn't see any sign of Will or anyone else. He turned to go back to the house. On the way he asked some of the cotton pickers he passed if they'd seen Will. But they all either ignored him or shook their heads and kept on picking.

When he asked Jeremiah if he had seen Will return from school, Jeremiah just shook his head.

"Wonder if he's around the school building. Let's go find out," Sam said to Moses as he climbed in the wagon.

"If you find him," Mrs. Cobb said, "please tell him his mama said to come right home."

"Let's jus' you and me drive back through town on the way to the school buildin' and keep us a look-out," Moses said.

Moses flicked the reins and the wagon lurched forward. Sam looked to the right and left side of the road as they drove down the long driveway of the Cobb farm and entered onto the main road. Sam could see nothing but fields for the first few miles. Then some hanging oak trees came into his view with a shack set back from the road. Sam remembered the shack from the day he and Will had initiated it as their secret meeting place.

"That looks like an awfully large dark moss hanging down from that tree," Sam commented. "Whoa!" Moses suddenly pulled the reins tight. "Don't look like no moss to me," he said.

Sam hopped down from his seat and walked over

to get a closer look. But as he neared the thing hanging—he knew it wasn't a hanging moss.

"I—i—it looks like a man."

Moses, who walked up behind Sam, took off his cap and knelt down before the hanging dark-skinned figure. "I knows 'im. Dat ders de man we's just selected our mayor." Tears ran down Moses' cheeks as he bowed his head. "Needs to git someone to cut 'im down and bury him decent like," he mumbled. "Come away, Sam, ain't nothin' nobody can do—he's dead. Lawd's me."

"I'll see if anyone in that shack over there can help us."

Sam walked over to the cabin and knocked on the door. He heard some shuffling inside. Will opened the door. When Will saw Sam, he quickly pulled the door closed behind him.

"What yuh doin' here?" Will slurred at Sam.

"Your mama's looking for you. I came to find you. Phew. What'cha got into, Will Cobb, bark juice[11]?"

Will picked up a shovel leaning against the wall. Then he lifted it over his head and lunged toward Sam. Sam backed away just in time. Will lost his balance and fell. Moses—who had by this time come up beside Sam—reached for the shovel just as the door opened and some older boys came through the door, stumbling over Will's prone form on the ground.

"Hey, Negro, you goin' be your nigger friend's grave digger? Noose'll be just warm 'nough fer your nigger head next."

"Git in the wagon, Sam," Moses ordered Sam. He backed up with the shovel still raised in the air. "Y'all best git on home if yuh can a'fore I bring de law back fer y'all."

One of the boys said, "Looky there, nigger your law is hanging." They laughed, stumbled and lurched toward Moses, who by this time was in the wagon beside Sam, had taken up the reins, and the wagon pulled away.

ALBERT ATTENDS THE MEETING

"You ain't goin' let dose bullies gits yuh, are yuh, Pappy?" Albert said at supper that night. Moses had dropped Sam off at the Kennesaw House and gone back to their cabin. He had told Albert and Sylvia all about finding the newly selected mayor hanging from the tree and being chased and sneered at by the white boys.

"We been always bullied and beaten. Dis de way it be, son."

"But Pappy, we's freed now."

Sylvia, Albert's mother sighed. "It be costly."

"But we gots a mule, a wagon and schoolin'," Albert said.

"If dey don't kill de school teacher," Moses said. "But we best git goin' to dat meetin' Reverend Benedict done called."

Sylvia said, "I's goin' stay wid de little ones fer Miss Benedict. Mattie you goin' come wid me." She looked at Albert and Moses. "You two go, but be careful."

Albert sat beside his father in the seat in front of the wagon. After leaving his mother and Mattie at the Kennesaw House, Mrs. Benedict, Sam and Emily climbed into the wagon. On their way to the meeting, they passed many others going in the same direction. Some linked arms and carried signs. *Free to Learn*, Albert read on one sign. Albert turned back and met Sam's eyes and grinned.

"We're learnin' together."

But when they neared the school where they were attending classes, Albert saw white hooded figures carrying flaming torches surrounding the building. Moses stopped the wagon at the bottom of the steps leading up to the front door. Sam jumped down while Albert helped Sam's mother and Emily step down. The three Benedicts walked up the steps and into the building. Albert started to follow Sam. One of the hooded figures moved to block his way. Albert stepped back toward the wagon. Moses dropped the reins and started after the hooded man, his whip raised. At that moment Reverend Benedict appeared at the front door.

"I've called this meeting to discuss the safety of our school pupils," he said in a commanding voice. "In the authority invested in me as the rector of St. James Church, all who are enrolled in this school, both children and adults, are welcome to enter."

The white hooded figure blocking Albert's path moved back with the others who stood menacingly on one side of the steps. Some members of the newly formed local Freedmen Association gathered on the other side. One of them carried the sign that read, *Free to Learn*.

Reverend Benedict folded his arms across his chest and turned to stare down the hooded figures. Mrs. Fletcher and Master Calhoun, his head wreathed by a bandage, came to stand beside him—one on each side.

With his way now clear, Albert moved one foot forward. His stomach didn't want to follow.

Fear blurred his vision, but he took one more step. The Freedmen on his right cheered him on. He quickly hurried up the rest of the steps into the open door. Sam and Emily were waiting for him. They linked arms and went into the room where the meeting would be held.

Mrs. Fletcher—her ballooning skirts brushing the ground—walked down the steps and moved close to where the first hooded figure stood.

"If any of you gentlemen have sons and daughters enrolled in our school, you are invited to attend the meeting, but please extinguish your torch first. And since you'll be able to see and speak better, why don't you just leave your hood outside as well."

No one moved to enter the building. The first hooded figure said in a low voice, "You'll get what's coming to you, nigger lover."

Mrs. Fletcher turned her back on the threatening man and motioned to the waiting crowd. "Plenty of seats inside." She picked up her hooped skirts and walked sedately up the steps.

Reverend Benedict and Master Calhoun walked

down to the bottom of the steps and stood in front of the white shrouded figures. Those who were still waiting to enter the building now walked safely up the steps into the school building. The Freedmen followed and the white hooded figures mounted their horses and rode away.

As soon as he was safely inside, Albert's knees started shaking and he said in a barely audible voice to Mrs. Fletcher, "I feels sick."

"Well, don't get sick on my nicely polished floor. Here, you can sit by the window."

She took Albert by the elbow and led him to a stool near the front of the room and whispered, "You were very brave out there."

As soon as he was seated by the window, Albert felt better.

The meeting room filled up and all the seats were taken. Those who couldn't find a seat stood against the wall. Reverend Benedict called the meeting to order and introduced Master Calhoun.

"Thank you all for coming to this meeting. As you read on the notice, we needed to postpone classes until our new schoolmaster could recover from his blow on the head. We're glad he could be here with us tonight. I regret that demonstration outside, but we're all safe inside now. Thank you, Freedmen, for backing me up out there."

Spontaneous applause went up from ebony and cinnamon-colored hands with a sprinkling of white hands joining them. Albert joined them from his seat in front.

Master Calhoun spoke next.

"Apparently, my plan to open these classes to anyone who wants to learn has caused anxiety among some of our residents. Some of the local boys who have not been attending school threw stones and rocks and one of the rocks happened to hit me." He touched his bandage. There were "aws" and sympathetic murmurings.

"Do any of you have any suggestions as to how we can ensure the safety of our pupils?"

Hands were raised and Master Calhoun began calling on them one by one.

"Yessir. I 'spects it be best for parents to walk dey chillens to and from school."

"And de grown'd ups—dey comes together," said another.

"Law says everybody gits to be school'd."

Reverend Benedict spoke up next. "But just maybe, not together—yet."

"What you mean?" Albert came to life again.

A white woman in the back of the room spoke up in an angry voice. "What he means is that we want you to stay in your place, nigger boy."

"Give your seat to the lady, boy. You go stand up in the back of the room where you belong," yelled another white man.

People turned around in their seats to see who had spoken. Some stood up. Albert looked over at Reverend Benedict to know what he should do. But Reverend Benedict just raised his hand and said, "All right, ladies and gentlemen. I prefer to explain to Albert here." He turned to talk to Albert. "You weren't feeling well. That's why Mrs. Fletcher gave you the seat by the window." He turned back to the gathered assembly. "Will one of you gentleman in the front of the room please give up your seat for the lady in the rear?"

A white-haired, dark-skinned man stood up and with his cap in his hand, turned slowly around and bowed to the white lady and moved to the back of the room. She swished to her seat not even thanking him. Instead, as she brushed past him she covered her face with her fan.

"What I meant, Albert," Reverend Benedict continued, "was that if we had some more volunteers to help Master Calhoun as teachers and aides besides Mrs. Fletcher, we could have two classes, one with just black students and one with white students…" There was a murmur of assent in the room. "…then everyone could have access to schooling."

Albert shuffled his feet and put his head on his hands and his heart sank. Going to school and being in the same class with Sam and Emily was like a dream come true. *I guess it was just a dream after all,* he thought.

"Us Freedmen jes might find us another teacher," a husky voice in the back of the room spoke up.

"I could help out several days," a white woman said, "used to teach at St. James Academy."

Several others stood up to volunteer.

"All those who just voiced a willingness to help, please plan to stay after this meeting. Now…"

The front door flew open and a man came running in crying out, "Fire—town—help—Mrs. Fletcher."

People stood up and hastily grabbed their coats.

WILL WITNESSES A HANGING

For Will most of the day had been a blur of flashing scenes. The scene he witnessed from the window of the shack that morning stuck in his mind.

Through the window I watched white hooded figures riding up with a man whose dark brown hands were tied behind his back. He was blindfolded and was sitting on a horse. One of the hooded figures tied a rope made with a noose on the end to a branch of the oak tree; another put the noose around the man's head and tightened it. I swallowed the gasp trying to come out of my mouth. The man squirmed and let out a cry when his horse was whipped. The horse bolted out from under him, leaving him hanging from the tree.

    I backed away from the window. I didn't want to look anymore. I didn't want slaves to be free but I didn't believe in hanging them either. Teaching them a lesson—beating them—that was different. I glanced over at the other boys who hadn't moved from where they were seated in the middle of the room. I guess they were too busy drinking from the brown jugs.

"Come on, Willy, have some of this here corn likker, it will grow hair on you." So I joined them and tried to forget what I had just seen. It didn't take long until I passed out. When I came to, I was lying on the ground outside the shack in my own vomit. I started to sit up, but my head felt so heavy I just rolled over and tried to sleep. I felt awful.

Now Will didn't feel much better, but he had managed to drag himself away from that place where the man hung dangling from the tree, but he didn't want to go home either. His mother would kill him if she knew he'd been drinking liquor. And he wasn't hungry, so he found a bale of cotton by the side of the road and, using it as a pillow, slept most of the afternoon. When he woke up, his stomach growled.

Gotta find something to eat, he thought. He wasn't sure where. Then he remembered that his friend Sam was staying at the Kennesaw House, but when he neared it he saw Sam climb in the wagon with his sister and mother.

Wonder where they're going? he thought, but he had no desire to follow—not just yet anyway. He was too weak and too hungry. Instead he went to the rear of the Kennesaw House and leaned against the building, hoping that the cook inside just might have some leftovers from supper. The back door wasn't locked. He carefully opened it and went inside. The cook was singing and kneading something that looked like bread on the table in front of her with her back to Will. On another table beside the back door he could see a bowl of fruit. While the cook was still absorbed in her bread making, Will reached for an apple and a few grapes from a bowl on the table nearest him, and then he quietly exited through the same door without the cook turning her head.

By this time night was closing in on figures heading in the direction where the wagon had gone with the Benedicts. Will followed them for awhile. When his legs wouldn't take him another step, he flopped down under a tree and fell asleep instantly.

Eerie shapes—flickering flames of light—thundering hooves. Will woke up and rubbed his eyes. No—not ghosts—only the hooded riders again with their flaming torches. Will dragged his body back into the darkness under the tree branches, afraid to move, afraid to speak, thinking of the Negro man on the horse and seeing his own limp body hanging from that same tree.

He cautiously looked again at the scene in front of him. *That house. They're riding around the house with their torches. Whose house? Not sure.* Will covered his mouth to prevent a scream. *The house—it's burning!* Will watched spellbound as the flames licked their way up the sides of the house. Most of the hooded men turned their horses and disappeared into the night darkness, but one of them stopped his horse, took off his hood and watched. Will covered his mouth again to prevent a gasp from exploding. He knew who it was.

When the familiar person finally rode off into the darkness, Will decided he better get home fast.

SAM WATCHES THE FIRE

Men formed a bucket brigade to bring water from a nearby creek to put out the fire. But it was too late. With Albert, Emily and Thomas Calhoun standing next to him, Sam watched as the flames devoured and demolished almost everything in the house.

"What will you do?" Emily asked the schoolmaster. "Weren't you staying there?"

"Yes. And our school books were in the house, too."

Emily took his hand and squeezed it. "Don't worry. We'll find some more."

Someone brought a stool for Mrs. Fletcher—sobbing into her lace handkerchief—so she could sit down. "Papa?" Sam asked his father who had gone over to put his arm around her.

"Yes, son?"

"Remember those cots we saw at the Kennesaw House. The ones the Union soldiers slept in? Maybe Master Calhoun could sleep there."

"And I'll give Widow Fletcher my bed," Emily said.

"And I hope she can fit into some of my dresses," Mama added.

"Thank you both kindly," Mrs. Fletcher looked up after blowing her nose, "but I think I'll stay with my daughter, Georgia. She has an extra room."

One of the Freedmen came over to where the Benedict family members stood. "And I think I know who set fire to this house," he said.

"I suspect the Klan members, but what can we do about it?" Papa answered.

"Find the sheriff," someone said.

"But we have no sheriff and no courthouse."

"And they just found the Mayor's body hanging from a tree on old man Horace's property...."

Sam looked from one to the other. He thought, *Mr. Horace lives not far from the Cobb farm.* He and Moses had seen a shack and the body hanging from the oak tree. Then he remembered that the shack was in the back of the Horace property.

One of the Freedmen nearby said, "Needs a decent burial. Soon's we bury him, we'll hold a trial. Law says we ken."

Folks had begun to scatter, so Sam's mother and father escorted the weeping Mrs. Fletcher to her daughter's house. Master Calhoun walked behind with Sam and Emily.

"You can have my books, Sam said to the school master. "Albert rescued them after General Sherman's soldiers set fire to our house. Papa says that his congregation at St. James Church promised to rebuild the house for us—but they haven't gotten very far. That's why we have to stay in the Kennesaw House."

WILL TELLS

White figures flying at me. Their eyes flaming with fire. Snakes crawling up my legs. I need to shake them off and fend off the flying figures. My legs are like lead.

Will woke up with sweat pouring off his body. He shook all over. He could hear his father swearing through the thin walls. He buried his head under the quilt, but it didn't help so he threw the coverlet off and rubbed his arms, trying to make the shaking go away.

"Mama!" he called.

"What is it, Will?" She sat down on the bed beside him and felt his forehead.

"What hurts?"

"Just a dream, I guess." He wanted to tell her about what he'd seen last night but he couldn't get the words to come out. Then he remembered the notice he'd seen through his stupor.

"H—h—how was the meeting?"

"It broke up because Mrs. Fletcher's house was on fire. She's staying with her daughter, Georgia. Too bad. She lost everything and so did the new schoolmaster. I saw you were in bed when I came home. I was worried about you because you weren't home when I went to the meeting."

"Oh. Well, it..." Will started to say that it served them right because the new school teacher wanted to mix up former slaves with him in the same classroom, but then he remembered the man hanging from the tree and he put his head in his hands instead.

"Sam asked about you. Said he missed you. Why don't you get dressed and come with me. I thought I'd take one of my dresses over to Mrs. Fletcher—see what else she needs."

Will didn't really want to see Sam, but he didn't want to go with the older boys either. They might hang out where those hooded figures could get him. It would be a safer option to get dressed and go with his mother.

Will and his mother stopped first at the Kennesaw House. Will saw Sam and his brothers shooting marbles by the front door. He stopped to watch while his mother went inside.

"Hi Will, want to join us?" John asked him.

"No. I'll just sit here and watch for awhile," Will answered.

When the game was over, Sam asked Will to go with him to see the train engine called the General. "It's out in back on a siding—resting, I guess, from the war." Sam turned to Will. "Remember when she was such a proud shiny engine?"

Will thought, *I wish I were dead.* He remembered the day he'd seen Henry and his father board the train pulled by that engine and how he wished he'd been old enough to go with them. Maybe then the Yankees would have killed him, too. Then he wouldn't be so miserable being still alive.

Sam's voice broke off his thought. "Hey, Will. Do you remember? You don't seem like the same Will I used to know back then. That rock you threw. It hit Master Calhoun. That was a bad thing to do."

"I didn't mean to hit him—rock just went the wrong place that's all."

"But shouldn't you have told him you're sorry?" Sam said.

Will shrugged his shoulders. Then finally said, "He's trouble."

"Why is it his fault? And why can't we be still be friends? Seems you don't want to be nice to anyone anymore."

"You haven't been around," Will answered, turning his head the other way.

"I can't help that. We weren't allowed to be here—until now. But I remember especially the noises and the smells of the Battle at Kennesaw Mountain. Do you?"

"I remember burying Henry. Then there's Papa—he's now a lunatic."

"I'm sorry." Will felt Sam's arm around his shoulder and didn't resist.

"Do you ever have nightmares?" Will asked his friend.

"Yes. All the time and every noise makes me jump. Do you too?"

"Had one last night. These white figures were coming at me—snakes crawling up my legs. Yuck."

"Like the white hooded men we saw last night at the school? Oh, I forgot, you weren't there. They came with their flaming torches and almost wouldn't let Albert go up the steps into the building, but Papa and Mrs. Fletcher stood up to them. They even threatened Mrs. Fletcher—then her house burned down."

"Oh?" Will acted surprised even though he had been there to see the house burn.

"Just the idea of Albert going to be in the same school as me—well that's not right," he said.

"Why?" Sam asked. By now the two boys were sitting on a bench in front of the railroad station.

"Because it isn't. He belongs in the fields with the other Negros."

"But he's our friend, remember? We all played together before the war."

"He was a slave back then and knew his place."

"He's free—just like you and me—he has the same rights..."

Will stood up. "He doesn't have the same rights as me and my family."

Sam sighed. "Well, after last night's meeting he may have to be in a different class than us."

"Well, that's better." Will sat back down again.

"Did you hear there's going to be a trial?" Sam changed the subject.

"No. When? About what?"

"Someone murdered the new mayor and someone burned Mrs. Fletcher's house down. That someone the

Freedmen think is the white hooded men we saw last night."

"Oh," Will said quietly. He saw them. *Should I tell? But they'll come after me too. No—Better not tell anyone,* he thought. *But maybe…* He had this nagging feeling that he should tell someone.

"I think I heard Mama calling. I better go." Will got up and headed back to the Kennesaw House.

"Mama—there's something…" Will started to say on the way back to the farm but then he stopped.

"Yes, Will. What is it?"

Will rubbed his hands together. He looked around to make sure no one was following them.

"Mr. Van Cleve, who lives down the road…"

"What about him?"

"Didn't he used to run that cotton mill that those Yankee soldiers burned down?"

"Yes. I guess he's pretty bad off now." The Cobb wagon stopped in front of their house.

"I saw him last night," Will said softly.

They went upstairs to their living quarters. While his mother was hanging up her bonnet, she turned to Will and laughed. "You were sleeping when I got home. You must have seen him in your dreams."

"But it wasn't a dream. He was there."

"Where?"

"When they burned the house down." There. He'd said it.

Will's mother sat down in the nearest chair and gave Will a puzzled look.

"When who burned the house down?"

"The white hooded horsemen. I saw Mr. Van Cleve. He took his hood off when the others rode away."

"But what were you doing there? I didn't see you."

Will hung his head. "I—was scared—they'd get me."

Will kneeled down and put his head in his mother's lap to muffle the sobs that came out in spite of all his efforts trying to hold them in.

"And they hung that Negro, too," he gasped.

SAM AND WILL VISIT A GRAVEYARD

The next day Will asked Sam to go with him to visit Henry's grave. Sam wondered why Will wanted him to go along to visit the cemetery, but decided not to pry. Lately, when he tried to talk to Will, Will had been surly or angry. But today, Will seemed different—almost like he was before the Great War—so Sam came along with him, glad to be asked to go with his old friend.

"Do you come here often?" Sam asked.

"No. But Mama does. She puts fresh flowers on his grave," Will answered.

"I miss Henry," Will said.

I wish I'd had an older brother to miss, Sam thought. He had always been the older brother to John, Ernest, George and Cleve, even Emily, although it seemed sometimes she was older because she liked to boss.

"What was it like? I mean what was it like having an older brother?"

"I dunno," Will answered. "I wanted to be near him and do the things he did." He paused. "And he sometimes got blamed for stuff I did."

"That's what happens to me," Sam said. "I get the blame for what John or Ernest do, or for not keeping them from doing bad stuff. Then, Papa tells me to be the good big brother."

When they reached the cemetery, Sam walked with Will down rows of stone markers until they found the marker with Henry's name. He wondered what he should do now. Should he stay with Will or leave him alone? He watched Will kneel down in front of one of the grave markers. Sam stood off to one side with his cap in his hand. He'd been to burial services with Papa and watched caskets lowered into the ground. Papa said to stand back so the family could be close to their loved one. Sam watched as family members tossed dirt into the grave after the casket was lowered and heard his father say, "Ashes to ashes, dust to dust."[12] But death was never the end of it. He heard Papa preach about the dead rising from their graves and the glory that was Heaven. Maybe Henry was still waiting in his grave for that to happen. He saw Will mumbling something. *Maybe he's talking to Henry,* Sam thought. He shivered. He wondered if he'd hear a spooky voice coming from the grave so he stood as still as he could get.

"Okay. Let's go," Will said, getting up and turning around.

"Did he...did he...talk to you?" Sam asked.

"Well, yes..." Will looked surprised. " I heard just that...talk to you."

"About what?"

"About what I saw."

"What did you see?" Sam asked.

"Those white hooded riders that hung that Negro from the tree."

"I saw him too, remember? You came after me with a shovel."

"I don't remember."

"Maybe because you smelled of bark juice, then fell."

"Ah…" Will hung his head. "Please don't tell Mama," he pleaded.

"But you need to tell someone because you know who murdered him. He was a friend of Moses, Albert's father."

"I don't know why I need to tell. Moses is only a nigger."

"But killing is wrong, Will Cobb," Sam said.

Sam saw Will look in the distance toward Kennesaw Mountain. As he turned to close the cemetery gate, Will said, "Plenty of killing those Yankees did over there."

And Rebels too, Sam thought. *There was that time before the great battle that Papa had taken me with him to visit the soldiers in the trenches. I remember the squishing sound my boots made in the mud as I followed Papa. Papa held up his white cassock so it wouldn't get muddy. We stopped at a spot under a tree near a trench. Papa asked me to find a flat board or rock while he talked to the sol-*

diers. I searched until I found one not covered with mud. I took it back to Papa and helped him set up his communion set. The very next day I heard the guns and…

"We won that battle," Will interrupted Sam's thought, "but lost the war."

"So what's the point when so many were killed? Does war make killing right?" Sam asked.

Will shrugged his shoulders.

"Maybe. I'd sure like to kill that Yankee soldier that killed my brother, Henry."

"The Bible says you shouldn't kill anyone. That makes battles and war wrong. It was wrong to hang that colored man and you saw who did it. That makes you a witness."

"But if I tell, those hooded men will come and hang me, too."

"Not if they're in jail."

"Who's going to make them go to jail?"

"The Freedmen's Association, that's who."

ALBERT ATTENDS THE HEARING

Albert asked his mother if he could go to the hearing at St. James Church, being held there because there wasn't a courthouse building standing.

"What yuh wants to do dat fer?" Mammy asked. "Y'all be standin' outside."

"But, Mammy, Sam done tells me he's goin' wid Will."

"Deys white and you's black. Mite not be safe place fer us coloreds."

But Albert's father finally convinced her. The day of the hearing, Albert went with his father and stood close to him in the back of the church.

"Dis here court's now in session," said the Negro Freedman sitting at a table placed in front of the church.

"Seys who?" responded one of the white men sitting in one of the front pews. "This here's no real court trial."

There was an angry murmuring in the church. Albert felt Pappy put his arm around him and hold him tight.

"The United States Government says that Freedmen's Associations can hold trials where there is no other legal authority," Master Calhoun stood up and answered.

The Freedman continued, "This here is a hearin' 'bout Robert's hangin'. I call first for any witnesses."

There was a long silence and some shuffling of feet. Then Mrs. Cobb stood up. Albert saw Will, who was sitting beside her, slouch down in the pew. She turned to Will and, grabbing him by his elbow, pulled him up beside her. Then she turned back to face the table. "My son, Will, saw the man being hanged."

A gasp went up from the people in the other pews. Albert watched as Reverend Benedict came over to where Mrs. Cobb and Will were standing and say something to Will, but Albert couldn't hear what he said. Then Reverend Benedict walked up to the table with Will and stood in front of the Freedmen conducting the hearing. One of the Freedmen took a Bible off the table and held it out to Reverend Benedict. Then he said to Will, "Now son, I want you to place your left hand on this Bible that Reverend Benedict will hold for you, then raise your right hand and repeat after me, 'I do solemnly swear to tell the truth, the whole truth and nothing but the truth so help me God.'"

Albert leaned forward so that he could hear Will repeat the words.

"Now tell us where yuh were and who yuh saw doin' the hangin'."

Reverend Benedict put the Bible down on the table and stood close to Will as he answered. "I was in the shack and I saw men on horses. They had white hoods over their heads."

The Freedman asked, "Did you see who dey were?"

"No, not then."

"If you did recognize any of these hooded men at another time, please tell us now," the Freedman continued.

Will turned around and slowly moved his eyes across the people sitting in the front pews. "Him," he said pointing to one of the white men sitting in one of the front row seats.

Albert turned to Moses, whose body had stiffened, and whispered, "Pappy, who's Will pointin' to?"

Moses said, "The man who used to take our cotton at the mill."

"Oh, him," Albert whispered back. "He was mean."

"Mr. Van Cleve. Please stand. You are under arrest," one of the Freedman at the table said.

Albert watched as other Freedmen converged on Mr. Van Cleve and started to take him into custody. But the other white men in the front pews held on to him and started fighting the Freedmen.

Reverend Benedict called out in a loud voice, "Gentlemen. There will be no fighting in this church! All of you stand aside." Reverend Benedict went over and took Mr. Van Cleve by the arm. "Mr. Van Cleve belongs to this parish. He can stay in my custody at the Kennesaw House next door."

The Freedman conducting the hearing banged a gavel and said, "The accused will be in Rever'nd Benedict's custody. This hearin's dismissed until tomorrow."

Albert saw Sam go over to speak to Will as the pews emptied. People who passed him on the way out the door were grumbling and shaking their heads. Albert and Pappy waited until everyone had left, then Albert held tightly to his father's hand as they made their way across the railroad tracks to their cabin.

"What will happen next, Pappy?" Albert asked.

SAM AND WILL

"That was a brave thing to do," Sam said to Will as they left the church. "Weren't you scared?"

"If your papa hadn't stood up there with me, I couldn't have done it," Will answered. "I didn't want to do it, but Mama said I wouldn't get rid of the nightmares until I told someone what I'd seen."

Just then two of the white men who had been sitting in the front pews and had been trying to protect Mr. Van Cleve came alongside Will and Sam. While one of them grabbed Will's arm, the second man kicked him in one leg.

"Traitor boy," a sinister voice said, "you better skedaddle if you know what's good for you."

"Ow!" Will reached down with one hand to feel his leg. Mrs. Cobb and Mrs. Fletcher, who were walking ahead of Sam and Will, turned just as Will started to fall. Sam grabbed Will's free arm to pull him back up. Will's mother rushed to his other side.

"Leave dat young'un alone!" Moses's voice boomed from behind.

The man who had been holding on to Will's arm

turned and spat at Moses' feet. The man who had kicked Will moved to one side and sneered. "Ses who, nigger man."

Mrs. Fletcher shouted after the two men, "You bullies! Picking on a young boy like that. You ought to be ashamed of yourselves."

Will half walked and half limped in between Sam and his mother up to the front door of the Kennesaw House.

"I d—d—don't want to go in there. If he's in there, he'll get me, too."

"I don't think Papa will let him," Sam answered.

Will heard shouting, and then a voice saying, "Now Billy, calm down."

"C—c—can we go in the back door?" Will asked.

His mother nodded to Mrs. Fletcher. The two women walked on either side of Sam and Will around the building to the back door of the hotel. The cook was waiting there to open the door.

"Is that man still in the front parlor?" Will asked her.

"No. Reverend Benedict has taken him up to the third floor and locked him in the same room where he was locked in by Sherman's officers."

After Will's wound had been tended to by his mother, he joined Sam and his brothers and sisters in the parlor.

SAM AND EMILY FIND THE NOTE

"Mama says we need to get on home because of Papa," Will said. "But what if those masked men come to our house tonight and set it on fire? Do you suppose your mama would let me stay here with you?"

"Let's ask our mothers. Maybe you can sleep with me in my bed. There are no empty rooms here anymore. Master Calhoun stays here now and…"

A loud crash splintered their conversation.

Sam lunged to grab his brother, Ernest. He pushed Ernest to one side just as a rock came through the window near where Ernest was playing. Sam felt sharp pricks on his leg. Emily screamed. John stepped back and Will just stood and stared at the rock.

Sam's mother came rushing in, holding her ballooning dress and petticoats up with one hand. She stepped around the rock and broken glass and lifted the shaking Ernest into her arms. Meanwhile, she said to Sam, "Lie still until we see if there are any splinters of glass in your legs." She gave Ernest to Will's mother and then carefully removing Sam's pants, she examined his legs.

"There's a piece of paper wrapped around the rock," Will said, pointing to the object in front of him.

"Well, so there is," Reverend Benedict said as he came into the room. He picked up the rock and unwrapped the paper. Sam watched his father's face as he read the note. Reverend Benedict looked at it, took a deep breath, and crumbled it into a ball."

"What did the note say, Papa?" John asked.

"Nothing to trouble you about, son. But we best get all this glass cleaned up so we don't get anyone else hurt." He gave the crumbled note to the house servant who had come in to sweep up the broken glass.

"Here, you can put this wad of paper with the glass in the trash basket."

"What do you suppose the note said?" Emily whispered to Sam and Will as they were climbing the stairs to their bedrooms after dinner. Sam had already persuaded his mother and Will's mother to allow Will to stay overnight.

"Let's find out," Will whispered back. "After the others have gone to bed, we can sneak down and look for the paper."

When Emily got to her room, she cupped her hands and whispered in Sam's ear, "Meet you at the back steps in an hour."

Sam's younger brothers were asleep, so the two boys lay side-by-side in Sam's bed and whispered to each other.

"Do your legs still hurt?" Will asked first.

"Not much. Does yours?"

"A little. Mama says that comes from the bruises, but no bones are broken," Will whispered back.

"At least they won't have to cut our legs off—like they do to soldiers." But Sam was sorry he'd said that when he remembered that Will's father had lost an arm as a soldier. He tried to change the subject to get Will to think about something else.

"What do you think will happen to Mr. Van Cleve? S'pose the Freedmen will hang him or just put him in jail?"

"Depends," Sam said.

"On what?"

"On what he's convicted of. You didn't see him at the hanging did you?"

"No. They all had hoods on. I only saw him when he took his hood off after the men set fire to Mrs. Fletcher's house," Will said.

The two boys continued their whispering until they heard a rustling by the door.

"I think that's Emily. Time to go," Sam said as he got up as quietly as he could and put on his slippers.

Once safely in the hall, Sam and Will followed Emily. The three of them crept as quietly as they could down the back stairs of the hotel. They looked all around the kitchen for the trash basket.

"There it is—in the corner," Emily said. "I see Mama's gloves on the table over there. I think I'll put them on since there's broken glass in the basket."

"Try that ball of paper. Maybe that's it." Sam

pointed to what looked like bunched up paper. Emily picked the wad carefully out of the waste basket, opened it and read,

---

Go back up North preacher man
Or we're coming to get you next.

KKK

Emily shivered. "Does that mean they're coming to get Papa? What will he do?"

Will's teeth started chattering.

"Are you cold?" Sam asked.

"N—n—no. Just seeing white sheeted ghosts coming after us. "

ALBERT WATCHES THE HEARING

Albert and Moses arrived early for the hearing the next day.

"Got to git us a seat," Albert said to his father. Albert hoped that today he could sit somewhere close to his friends instead of standing in the back. He looked around.

"They ain't here yet, Pappy."

"Who?"

"Sam and Will—oh, here dey come," Albert said pointing toward the door of the church. Reverend Benedict came first holding onto Mr. Van Cleve's elbow. Mrs. Benedict and Mrs. Cobb followed with Sam, Will, John, and Emily. Mrs. Fletcher and Master Calhoun came in behind them. Albert waited until Sam and Will were seated.

"Com'on, Pappy, let's you and me sit behind 'em." Albert led the way and entered the pew row behind his friends and sat down with his father beside him.

"Move outta here niggers! Get back there where you belong," a big burly white man demanded.

Albert started to stand up, but Moses pulled him back down. Mrs. Fletcher, who had just sat down in a pew seat on the opposite side of the church, stood up, put her hands on her hips and went out into the aisle to confront the man who demanded that Albert and Moses move. She pointed her finger in the man's face and said, "They have just as much right to sit where they are as I do to sit where I am now sitting."

"With all due respect Ma'am," the man said, "No. They don't."

The two of them stood in the aisle and glared at each other. They seemed to have forgotten about Albert, who sat glued to his seat, trying hard to not move a muscle, while staring wide-eyed at the arguing adults.

Meanwhile, Sam and Will turned and noticed that Albert and Moses were sitting behind them. Albert nodded. Sam reached out his hand toward Albert. Will just frowned and turned back.

The Freedman who had been seated at the head of the table the day before sat down at the table again and was joined by another Freedman. A man dressed in uniform came to stand at attention beside the table.

"Dis here hearin' will now come to order. I've ask'd dis Feder'l Marshal…" he pointed to the man in uniform, "to keep y'all in order." He glared at the two standing facing each other. The Federal Marshall started down the aisle toward them. The big white man grumbled and went to sit on the other side of the church. Mrs. Fletcher went back to her seat after first patting Albert on the arm and whispering in his ear, "We don't give in to threats."

Albert watched Reverend Benedict push Mr. Van Cleve to stand in front of the desk. The head Freedman said, "Mr. Van Cleve, Will Cobb here done sed dat he sees you setting Mrs. Fletcher's house on fire. What yuh gots to say 'bout dat?"

"I didn't put my hand to set a fire."

"Why were you there?"

"I'm the Night Hawk[13] of our Klan. It was my duty to be there with the rest of my Klansmen. The Constitution of the United States gives us the right of free assembly. I was doing nothing wrong."

Albert heard some cheers from those in the audience. Then he listened as Reverend Benedict asked the Freedman if he could speak directly to Mr. Van Cleve. The Freedman nodded. Reverend Benedict said, "Billy. Do you consider deliberately burning down someone's house and hanging to be law abiding activities?"

"Well, Reverend, it wasn't right for the Federal Government to disregard our Confederate States rights. We need to uphold our southern honor."

Albert turned to his father and whispered, "What's he mean?"

"Shh, listen."

"We thanks you, Rever'nd. Now, Mr. Van Cleve, did you agree with your Klansmen that they should set fire to Mrs. Fletcher's house and hang our newly selected mayor?"

Albert sat on the edge of his seat as Mr. Van Cleve

pulled back his shoulders, raised them, tucked in his chin and said, "I ain't admitting to nothing in front of this farce of a court." Then, he spat on the floor.

The Federal Marshall came forward and put handcuffs on Mr. Van Cleve and said, "You are in contempt, sir. Since you are being disrespectful of this hearing, I'm placing you under custody of the United States Government. You'll get your chance to defend yourself in front of a federal court."

Everyone stood up. Some of the white men in the audience jeered at the Federal Marshall as he led Mr. Van Cleve out of the church. Albert leaned toward the pew in front of him to talk to Sam.

"Mr. Van Cleve used to whip us if we didn' have our cotton quota."

Moses added, "'bout time we gits some justice. Let's us go on home, son."

SAM GOES FOR HELP

Boom. Sam jumped and tried to hide under the pew nearest to the door of the church. Every loud noise still made him jump, even though Papa had reassured him that the Great War was over.

"Just thunderin'," Moses said as he and Albert passed by on their way out of the church. "Be rainin' soon."

Sam swallowed, straightened himself up, and joined Will who was outside the door waiting for him.

"Sounded like a cannon ball," Sam mumbled. He blushed and averted looking directly at Will.

"Race you back to the Kennesaw House...see if we can beat the rain," Will said.

Sam turned to ask his father if he was coming with them.

"Go ahead, boys," Reverend Benedict said. "I have to stay and close up." He headed back into the building.

Sam glanced up at the darkening sky. Meanwhile Will had started running and Sam had to run fast to catch up. They both arrived at the front door of the Kennesaw House at about the same time. But Sam reached out and touched the door just five seconds before Will. At that moment another clap of thunder sounded and the first big drops of rain hit the pavement behind them.

"Beat you," Sam said when he could catch his breath.

"Where's Papa?" Emily, who had arrived earlier with her mother, asked when she opened the door.

"He's coming," Sam said as he flopped down on the nearest chair. Mama was just coming down the stairs.

"Will, your mother said as soon as the storm is over, you're to go on home," Mrs. Benedict said to Will.

An hour later when the sun had begun to peek through the rain clouds and it was time for Will to leave for home, Sam asked his mother why Papa still hadn't returned from locking up the church.

"Wonder what's keeping him?" Mama said. "Supper's almost ready. Sam, you go with Will as far as the church when he leaves to see about your papa."

So Sam walked with Will then waved good-bye when Will continued down the road toward home. Thinking that his father may have locked the door, Sam knocked—timidly at first. Hearing no answer, he turned the knob. To his surprise the door opened.

"Papa?" he called. He listened for a response, but only heard a faint moan coming from the direction of the sacristy.[14]

"Papa! Are you here? Where are you?" Sam called again. Panic gripped his chest. He rushed up the side aisle, past the pews and opened the sacristy door. He gasped when he saw his father lying face up on the floor and making moaning sounds. Blood trickled down on to his white collar. His face looked like someone had used it as a punching bag. Sam gasped. Then his father tried to speak.

"They jumped me—too many—hurt bad."

"Can you sit up?"

Sam leaned over and put his arm around his father's shoulders to help him sit up.

"Ouch! C—can't. Get your mother."

Sam retrieved a cassock[15] from the closet, rolled it up and put it under his father's head. Then he ran as fast as he could from the church to the Kennesaw House. When he reached the door to the hotel, he knocked loudly and said, "Open up. Come quick! Papa's been hurt." A servant opened the door and called for Mrs. Benedict, who, after she heard the story from Sam, grabbed her shawl. "How bad? What happened?"

"He's on the floor in the sacristy—can't sit up. His face is bleeding and swollen."

"We'll need something to carry him on, like a stretcher," said Master Calhoun, who by this time had heard the commotion and had come downstairs. "Think I saw some of those at the Military Institute. Sam, run to Albert's house and see if Moses can take the wagon to fetch one of those stretchers. Meanwhile, Emily, get some rags from the cook, water and a blanket and bring them to the church."

"I'll find the Doctor," Mrs. Fletcher said.

Master Calhoun followed Mrs. Fletcher and Sam's mother while Sam ran across the railroad tracks over to Albert's cabin.

ALBERT ASKS

Albert was eating his supper of greens, yams, and ham hocks when Sam arrived. Albert heard a knock on the door just as he finished saying to Mammy, "Dat mean man can't hurt us no mo'."

Sam called frantically through the closed door, "Moses! Albert! Papa's hurt—need wagon—stretcher!"

Moses rose from his place at the table and unlocked the door. When Albert saw Sam's wide-eyed look and heard about Reverend Benedict lying all bruised and bleeding at the church, he rushed outside to hitch up the wagon. While Albert climbed up on the wagon to help his father, Sam jumped in beside him. When they reached the building that was now the new school, the three of them scattered to look through the rooms for stretchers. Albert found two of them on the second floor in one of the rooms he had been searching. Beside them were piled cots and torn confederate uniforms, bandages and old bottles. He helped Moses and Sam carry one of the stretchers and some of the bandages to the wagon. Then Moses drove the wagon back to the church building where they found Doc Feltwell examining Reverend Benedict.

"Seems they beat you up pretty bad. Maybe a couple of cracked ribs and bruises," the doctor was saying to Mrs. Benedict. "Didn't get your teeth knocked out—that's the good news."

Albert, Sam and Moses gave Doc Feltwell the stretcher and some bandages.

"Ah," the doctor said. "Just what we need to patch you up and get you over to the Kennesaw House for some proper bed rest and care.

Albert watched as Doc Feltwell wrapped bandages around Sam's father's chest and head. Then Master Calhoun, Moses, and the doctor, with Sam's help, lifted him carefully up onto the stretcher. Sam, Emily and Albert followed the stretcher out of the church.

"Who done dat to yer papa?" Albert asked Emily who was standing by crying.

"Papa told us that four men in white hoods came into the sacristy while he was removing his cassock and beat him 'till he blacked out," Emily said between her tears.

"What dey do dat fer?" Albert asked. Emily just wiped her eyes and shrugged her shoulders.

Moses drove the wagon with Reverend Benedict on the stretcher back to the hotel, then helped Master Calhoun and Doc Feltwell carry his stretcher up the stairs so as not to upset him. They gently lifted him onto his bed.

Albert was waiting in the wagon when Moses returned. He sat silently beside his father as he maneuvered their wagon back across the railroad tracks to their cabin.

Finally, Albert turned to ask,

"Why dose men do dat?"

Having not received an answer when he asked Emily the same question, Albert said, "Rever'nd—he good man. Deys bad mens to do dat."

Moses, too, was silent. Then he turned to Albert and said,

"Son, deys white men who thinks deys still fighting 'gainst us bein' set free. Deys real angry—mean angry—scary angry."

"Dey can't make us slaves ag'in, can dey, Pappy?"

"Hopes not, son, hopes not."

Albert certainly didn't want to go back to the way it was before the war but he was scared. He reached out his hand to touch his father and moved over closer. *At least,* he thought, *my big strong Pappy will keep on protecting me so I don't lose no hope.*

SAM AND HIS FRIENDS

Sam's papa had to stay in bed through three Sundays of services at St. James. Sam took turns with Emily taking meals up to Papa.

One day when he was sitting up in bed, Papa said to Sam, "Thank you, son. This reminds me of the time you and Will brought me food from home when I was locked up by General Sherman. Now it's not the union army officers who are punishing me, its members of my own flock." He sighed.

Sam wondered what Papa meant. He seemed so sad. Then he remembered that Mr. Van Cleve was a member of St. James before the War and he was one of them—the white-hooded horse riders with the flaming torches. *Were there more of them and why would they want to hurt Papa?* Sam thought. Once again he wished they were back in Canada where there weren't so many dangers lurking.

While Papa was recuperating at the Kennesaw House, Sam, with Emily and John, accompanied by Master Calhoun and Mrs. Fletcher, walked every day to their classes at their new school. Sam, Emily, and John were assigned to a room on one side of the building with Master Calhoun as their teacher, while Albert and the other coloreds were assigned to a room across the hall with Mrs. Fletcher as their teacher. Will, who now had to attend school because his mother became a teacher's aide, sat next to Sam. But Sam was disappointed that he and Albert had to be segregated into separate classes.

"Why couldn't all three of us be friends just like we were before the war?" he asked his mother. She had sighed and said,

"That's just the way it is, Sam, in order to prevent any more violence."

After Sam's father could sit up in bed and take a few steps, he walked with Sam's mother on one side and Sam on the other. The swelling on his face had gone down and his wounds were healing over.

One Saturday, while Sam and his mother were walking with him, Mama asked Papa,

"We'll need to move out of here soon. When will the congregation at the church finish repairing the old rectory[16]?"

Papa shook his head. "They won't. Not enough money. Besides, it will be safer for the whole family if we find a house away from town."

"Can Albert and his family come with us?" Sam asked.

"That depends," Mama said. "Remember they have the freedom to choose now. We can't tell them what to do. But we'll ask them."

"What about school?" Sam continued. "Will we have to go to a new school?"

But his father was tired of walking and talking, so he asked to lie down again in his bed. As soon as he had settled himself, he turned to Sam and answered his last question, "I don't think so. At least for now. You, Emily, and John can ride in the wagon with me every day. I might even do some teaching at the new school when I'm well enough."

Since Papa wasn't well enough to join her in looking for a new house to live in, Sam's mother left the younger children and Lucy with Sylvia while Sam, John and Emily were in school. Moses drove her around the countryside to look for a new home.

WILL ATTENDS SCHOOL

Will stayed close to his house after the trial and Reverend Benedict's beating. He didn't have as many nightmares as before, waking up in a cold sweat with white hooded men chasing him with flaming torches.

For the first week after the trail, the older boys who had been with Will at the time of the hanging came and asked him to go out with them, but Will just shook his head, no.

"Hey, Will, you scaredy cat," they jeered, "guess you just not growed up."

Those comments made Will mad. Of course he wasn't grown up. What did they think? And the memories of seeing that body hanging from the tree and how awful he felt drinking that bark juice gave him courage to ignore their jeers. After a few times of trying to get Will to go with them and Will declining, the older boys left him alone.

Now that he wasn't hungry all the time, Will could think about other things besides filling his stomach.

He thought about how his world had turned upside down since the Great War. His family was now poor. His mother had to work. She kept telling Will how much she was counting on him to learn as much as he could so that he could help with the farm. They no longer could own slaves, so they had to find workers to tend the cotton fields. *Where was the money to come from to pay them?* Will wondered. He still couldn't accept that Negros couldn't be expected to work for them without pay, but as long as they stayed in their place, he was okay with them being free. He still didn't want to sit in the same classroom with Albert and the other former slaves. Yet they had a right to learn to read and write, just as he did, if they showed proper respect.

Will prayed that Papa would suddenly get well and stop shouting and screaming so much. Sometimes he had to put cotton in his ears to sleep at night. He didn't know how Mama could stand his swearing and yelling. When she began to help as a teacher's aide in the new school, Will was glad she could get away, but when she insisted that he come with her to school every day, he resisted. But finally he had to give in. Anyway, he didn't really want to stay around the house all day alone. *Besides,* he thought, *it will only be for half a day and that gives me more time to hang out at home in the afternoons—at least until Mama gives me chores to do on the farm.*

"Idle hands are the devil's workshop," Mama said.

Will's mother arranged with Jeremiah to oversee some of the former slaves to tend the fields in return for continuing to live on the farm property. With some order restored in his life, Will's bitterness mellowed.

Eventually, Will found he liked the classes at his new school and Master Calhoun was a pretty decent teacher.

But it was Sam's family's plans to move away that most upset Will. When Sam told him they would be moving out of the Kennesaw House and into their new home in the country on the opposite side of Marietta from where Will lived, Will didn't know how he could get along without his friend.

"We'll still see each other at school every morning," Sam said when Will complained how unhappy he was about Sam moving so far away. "Maybe we can play *Around Town* some afternoons when Papa has to stay late. Then you can visit me and I can visit you," Sam replied.

ALBERT ACCEPTS

"What we goin' do when Benedicts done move?"

Even thinking about what it would be like with his friend Sam's move away upset Albert.

"Well, Miss Benedict done asks us to come if we chooses to come," his father replied. "Says de new place at Flat Shoals has room fer all of us."

"She done need help wid all dose chillens," Sylvia said.

"Still we got dis here cabin and dat land de Freedmens done gave us to farm," Moses said scratching his head. "Massa Benedict, he done built dis cabin hisself and now it's ours. Massa say so."

"But we're family wid Benedicts, Pappy," Albert pleaded. "I wants to go where dey goes."

Mattie nodded.

"Den der's school wid Master Calhoun," Pappy said.

Albert realized how proud his father was to be able to write his name now that he attended the evening class. *Pappy's schooling could continue, but my dream of learning together with Sam in the same class won't happen*, he thought.

Sylvia shook her head. Albert watched her as she looked from him to his father and then back again. Albert had a sense that she wanted to go and live with the Benedicts like he did, but knew how important it was for Moses to be able to learn to read and write and farm his own land.

His mother finally stated her compromise between their choices.

"Maybe we lives here and helps when dey needs us."

"And Sam and I can still play *Around Town* and shoot marbles together at their new home." Albert felt better now. Yet, he still couldn't be friends with Will and would have to keep a respectful distance. He sighed with the reality of his acceptance. Someday he would be truly free.

EPILOGUE

Sam did move with his family to a place called Flat Shoals because not only was it dangerous for his father to stay in Marietta but also the church congregation could no longer afford to pay for his services. Reverend Benedict left St. James Church and assumed a new position as pastor and preacher at St. John's Church in Savannah while the rest of the family stayed in the country farther away from marauding Ku Klux Klan lynchings and beatings. When Albert came with his family to help out at Flat Shoals, Sam and Albert were able to maintain their friendship. Sam and Will attended classes at school in the morning and played together in the afternoons, parting when it was time for Sam to climb onto his father's wagon. Eventually, an all white private school started closer to Sam's new home and he and Will drew apart. After Thomas Calhoun returned to his northern home, Albert and former slave children were segregated into an all black public school taught by educated Negros. Albert did fulfill his dream of becoming a teacher after attending an all black college in the South. Georgian schools remained segregated well into the twentieth century.

Will's father never recovered. The blue pills commonly given to wounded soldiers for controlling pain during the Civil War destroyed brain cells and made hair and teeth fall out. When Will took over managing the farm, he hired many of their former slaves as share-croppers and they were no better off than they had been as slaves. It was many years after the end of the Civil War that southern families like Will's finally accepted former slaves as equals.

Therefore, issues of racial discrimination were not resolved in my great grandfather's generation. . Nor was the issue resolved in my grandfather's generation, nor in his childrens'—my father's generation. Jim Crow laws and continued segregation in schools, public transportation, restrooms and private establishments kept African-Americans from achieving real freedom. Perhaps we have seen a glimpse of real freedom and acceptance for all America's citizens in this new millennium. Maybe America can finally become that perfect union for which so many have longed.

Excerpts from three speeches follow: The first, from Abraham Lincoln's Second Inaugural Address in 1865; the second, by that courageous statesman who was a spokesperson for all newly freed slaves at that time, Frederick Douglass, in 1866, two years before the setting of this story; the third, from then Senator Barack Obama in Philadelphia one hundred and forty two years later.

With malice toward none; with charity for all, with firmness in the right, as God gives us to see the right, let us strive on to finish the work we are in, to bind up the nation's wounds, to care for him who shall have borne the battle and for his widow and his orphan, to do to all which may achieve and cherish a just and lasting peace among ourselves and with all nations.

—Abraham Lincoln's
Second Inaugural Address, March 4, 1865

Fortunately, the Constitution of the United States knows no distinction between citizens on account of color. Neither does it know the difference between a citizen of a State and a citizen of the United States. Citizenship evidently includes all the rights of citizens, whether State or national. If the Constitution knows none, it is clearly no part of the duty of the Republican Congress now to institute one. The mistake of the last session was the attempt to do this very thing, by a renunciation of its power to secure political rights to any class of citizens, with the obvious purpose to allow the rebellious States to disfranchise, if they should see fit, their colored citizens. This unfortunate blunder must now be retrieved, and the emasculated citizenship given to the negro supplanted by that contemplated in the Constitution of the United States which declares that the citizens of each State shall enjoy all the rights and immunities of citizens of the several States.–so that a legal voter in any State shall be a legal voter in all the States.

—Frederick Douglass, "Reconstruction",
Atlantic Monthly 18 (1866): 761–765.

Legalized discrimination—where blacks were prevented, often through violence, from owning property, or loans were not granted to African-American business owners, or black homeowners could not access FHA mortgages, or blacks were excluded from unions, or the police force, or fire departments—meant that black families could not amass any meaningful wealth to bequeath to future generations. That history helps explain the wealth and income gap between black and white, and the concentrated pockets of poverty that persists in so many of today's urban and rural communities.

A lack of economic opportunity among black men, and the shame and frustration that came from not being able to provide for one's family, contributed to the erosion of black families—a problem that welfare policies for many years may have worsened. And the lack of basic services in so many urban black neighborhoods—parks for kids to play in, police walking the beat, regular garbage pick-up, building code enforcement—all helped create a cycle of violence, blight and neglect that continues to haunt us…

… But I have asserted a firm conviction—a conviction rooted in my faith in God and my faith in the American people—that working together, we can move beyond some of our old racial wounds, and that in fact we have no choice if we are to continue on the path of a more perfect union.

For the African-American community, that path means embracing the burdens of our past without becoming victims of our past. It means continuing to insist on a full measure of justice in every aspect of American life. But it also means binding our particular grievances—for better health care, and better schools, and better jobs—to the larger aspirations of all Americans—the white woman struggling to break the glass ceiling, the white man who's been laid off, the immigrant trying to feed his family. And it means also taking full responsibility for our own lives—by demanding more from our fathers, and spending more time with our children, and reading to them, and teaching them that while they may face challenges and discrimination in their own lives, they must never succumb to despair or cynicism; they must always believe that they can write their own destiny…

…In the white community, the path to a more perfect union means acknowledging that what ails the African-American community does not just exist in the minds of black people; that the legacy of discrimination—and current incidents of discrimination, while less overt than in the past—are real and must be addressed. Not just with words, but with deeds—by investing in our schools and our communities; by enforcing our civil rights laws and ensuring fairness in our criminal justice system; by providing this generation with ladders of opportunity that were unavailable for previous generations. It requires all Americans to realize that your dreams do not have to come at the expense of my dreams; that investing in the health, welfare, and education of black and brown and white children ultimately help all of America prosper.

Costly Freedom

In the end, then, what is called for is nothing more, and nothing less, than what all the world's great religions demand—that we do unto others as we would have them do unto us. Let us be our brother's keeper, Scripture tells us. Let us be our sister's keeper. Let us find that common stake we all have in one another, and let our politics reflect that spirit as well...

—Barack Obama,
excerpts from speech in Philadelphia,
March 18, 2008.

BIBLIOGRAPHY

Primary Sources

Agle, Nan Hayden. *Free to Stay.* Arcadia Enterprises, Inc. Salisbury, MD. 2000.

Batteryb.com/terms.html. *Common Words of the 1860s.* Retrieved December 30, 2008.

Baumgartner, Richard A. *Kennesaw Mountain June 1864.* Blue Acorn Press. Huntington, W. Va. 1998.

Burial Service, *Book of Common Prayer of the Protestant Episcopal Church.* Charles E. Eyre and William Spottswoode, New York, NY. 1862.

Denenburg, Barry. *When will this Cruel War be over? The Civil War Diary of Emma Simpson.* Scholastic, New York. 1996.

Doctorow, E.L. *The March.* Random House. 2005.

Em.wikipedia.org/wik/Ku_Klux_Klan. Retrieved November 22, 2006. <http://emWikipedia.org>

Georgiaencyclopedia.org/nge/article. Retrieved March 3, 2009. <Http://www. Georgiaencyclopedia.org>

Hepburn, Julia Benedict. "Some things that I remember myself and stories that were told to me." (oral/written family history)

Higgins, Henry and Cox, Connie with Anderson, Jean Cole, *Journal of a Landlady,* eds Professional Press. Chapel Hill, NC 1995.

Horton, James Oliver and Horton, Lois. *Slavery and the Making of America.* Oxford University Press. New York, NY. 2005.

Library.thinkquest.org/J0110166/marbles.htm. Retrieved August 20, 2008. http://.www.Library.thinkquest.org

Obama, Barack. *The Audacity of Hope.* Vintage Books ed. July, 2008.

Paden, Rebecca Nash and McTyre, Joe. *Images of America: Cobb County.* Arcadia Publishing. Chicago , Il. 2005.

Pbs.org/wgbh/amex/reconstruction/nast/sf_nast_09.html. Retrieved March 13, 2009. <http://www.pbs.org>

Pearsall, Shelley. *Trouble Don't Last.* Alfred A. Knopf. New York, NY. 2002.

Robins, Glenn. *The Bishop of the Old South: The Ministry and Civil War Legacy of Leonidas Polk.* Mercer University Press. Macon, GA. 2006.

Shampp, Kenneth M. *The Era of Reconstruction 1865–1877.* Vintage Books, Random House. New York. 1965.

Smith, Page. *Trial by Fire: A People's History of the Civil War and Reconstruction,* (5) McGraw-Hill. 1982.

Stowe, Harriet Beecher. *Uncle Tom's Cabin.* Bantam Books. 1981.

Secondary Sources

Personal visit to Marietta, Georgia to search archives in St. James Church, Kennesaw Battle Museum and Marietta Museum

Visited the following Internet Sources:

nwinfo.net/~jagriffin/jatucker.htm

stjamesmarietta.com/Main_Page_our_history.php

docsouth.unc.edu/benedict/benedict.html

ngeorgia.com/travel/kennesawmtn.html

digitalhistory.uh.edu/reconstruction

your dictionary.com/library/southernese

ENDNOTES

1 Suitcases.

2 Knapsack.

3 A form of baseball.

4 An outdoor cape worn by clergy over vestments.

5 The kind of cap confederate soldiers from Georgia wore.

6 Carpetbaggers were white Northerners who went south after the beginning of the Civil War. Sooner or later, they became active in politics, became teachers, clergymen and officers of the Freedmen's Bureau.

7 These were made of Mercury Chloride which is a poison that went right to the brain, made the victim's teeth and hair fall out and turned them crazy.

8   Bags made of hemp or burlap, called gunnysacks except in the south.

9   Someone who believed slavery should be abolished legally.

10 Song: Smith, *Trial By Fire*, p. 601

11 Whisky.

12 From the 1862 Book of Common Prayer belonging to Reverend Benedict's father.

13 Term used for the official in charge of security.

14 A room where pastors changed into their robes for the service and where the communion elements were being kept.

15 Vestment worn by some clergy.

16 House owned by churches for clergy families to live in. They were often attached to church buildings.

listen|imagine|view|experience

AUDIO BOOK DOWNLOAD INCLUDED WITH THIS BOOK!

In your hands you hold a complete digital entertainment package. Besides purchasing the paper version of this book, this book includes a free download of the audio version of this book. Simply use the code listed below when visiting our website. Once downloaded to your computer, you can listen to the book through your computer's speakers, burn it to an audio CD or save the file to your portable music device (such as Apple's popular iPod) and listen on the go!

How to get your free audio book digital download:

1. Visit www.tatepublishing.com and click on the e|LIVE logo on the home page.
2. Enter the following coupon code:
   4d15-3e51-2576-838f-a8f4-579d-69c7-d6c0
3. Download the audio book from your e|LIVE digital locker and begin enjoying your new digital entertainment package today!